FINAL ART TK

1

I NEVER THOUGHT I'D end up trapped in Albert Einstein's dog crate tonight, teetering at the top of our basement stairs. But you know, it only proves my point. Like I always tell my friend Joon: bad stuff can pop up and trap you at any time.

I mean, even if it seems like stuff is going okay? Suddenly, wham, just like in the comics: a splash page of heart-thumping action can explode out of nowhere. Pow! One minute, you're happily eating a piece of cake. Boom! The next minute? Dog crate of doom.

It all started because my brother, Calvin, turned fourteen today. We had pot roast, gravy, and a giant vat of mashed potatoes that Cal basically inhaled single-handedly. It was just the four of us: me, Gramps, Mom, and

Cal. And Albert Einstein, under the table. That's our dog—the world's least intelligent golden retriever.

Mom got off work early for the first time in months so she could cook Cal's favorite birthday dinner. She also made this amazing chocolate birthday cake. Three layers. Frosting like melt-in-your-mouth fudge.

So, after dinner, once Mom had gone back out for a real-estate showing . . . I decided to steal another hunk of it.

But Cal must have heard me sneak into the kitchen. Because all of a sudden—wham!—he leapt out of thin air. He slammed his hand on the counter so hard, both the cake plate and I jumped.

"Illegal cake grab, Stanley!" Cal shouted. "My birthday, MY CAKE!"

I froze. Freezing was a bad choice because Cal had me in an instant headlock.

"Let me go, Cal!"

Just like certain superheroes, there are times when I have to set aside my usual commitment to nonviolence. This was one of those times. I stomped on Cal's foot, hard as I could. His grip loosened! I ducked, spun, and twisted free—I was getting away! I dashed behind him— but now I was trapped in a corner. Stupid, stupid, stupid!

An evil grin unfurled across Cal's slightly hairy face. "Got you now," he growled.

I looked around, frantic. Albert Einstein's dog crate! I flung open the wire mesh door and dashed inside. Cal lunged—but he was too late. I scrambled to the back and scrunched up into a tiny ball, as far from his groping hands as I could get.

I was safe!

Or so I thought.

Because then, the crate door slammed shut. And I was being slid along the floor, toward the top of the basement stairs.

"Stop screaming, you weenie," said Cal. "I'm not gonna push you down the stairs." Then he giggled. When Cal giggles, it sounds like the squeak of a rusty metal gate hinge: "HEEEE! HEEEE! HEEEE!" And sometimes he throws in a snort, like a pig's stuck in that rusty gate. "SNORT! HEEEE!"

"Nooo!" I hollered.

But yes.

Cal placed the back half of the crate, with me in it, on firm ground. But the front half he left hanging over the top step. So now, if I scramble forward to open the door, I'll unbalance—and crash down into the basement.

I try not to think about that. I hug my knees and stay still as a statue. My glasses are smudged with chocolate, but I can't risk taking them off to polish them. I can't risk any movement at all. I try not to hyperventilate.

Cal grabs my cake plate and brings it over near me. He sits cross-legged by my cage. "Mmmmmm," he says, spewing crumbs, rolling his eyeballs around. "Delicious!"

I have this stack of comics upstairs two feet high. In any one of them, the hero or even the sidekick would be out of this bind in a flash. Superman would melt the bars. Batman would open his crazy utility belt. The Flash wouldn't have gotten caught in the first place. Wolverine would be out with one swipe of a claw. Spidey would sling a web and drag himself to safety.

But I'm no superhero. I'm about as far from a superhero as you could find. The only thing I can do is huddle in the corner of this dumb crate and feebly croak: "HELP!"

4

2

NOT A MOMENT too soon, Mom comes in the back door. She stands there in her bright red real estate blazer, rubbing her nose and gaping at us. "What on earth? What's going on, here? CALVIN?" Mom dumps an armload of folders on the table, and suddenly Calvin's morphed from Mr. Evil to Mr. Helpful, lending a hand to drag the crate back onto solid ground. I keel over inside it, still curled in a ball, and wait for my heart to stop hammering.

"Why are you in that crate, Stanley? Calvin, why is Stanley in the crate?"

Mom looks exhausted. Her face is pale. She pinches the bridge of her nose with her fingers and closes her eyes. "Wait. You know what? I don't want to know."

"Mom!" I protest. "You do want to know!"

"Aw, Ma!" Cal laughs like the Most Reasonable Boy in the World. "It's just, you know, boys being boys! And you have to admit, isn't that pretty cool, how I set up the crate? See how he couldn't get out? Pretty clever, huh?"

"Calvin Fortinbras, you're fourteen years old. Next year, Lord help us, you will be in high school. And this is how you choose to spend your time?"

As Cal slinks away, she falls into a kitchen chair, sighing, and kicks off her high heels.

"Aren't you going to ground him or something?" I say, climbing cautiously out of the crate.

"I'll deal with him later," Mom says, rubbing her toes.

I start to leave the room, but Mom clamps one of her iron claw-hands down on my shoulder. She turns me to face her, and gives me The Look. The one where her eyes glow like lasers, boring into your very soul. "You're breathing fast, Stanley. How are you feeling? Really?" She feels my forehead.

"I'm fine."

Mom frowns at me for a long moment. Finally, she releases me. She struggles to her feet and goes to rinse the stack of plates in the sink. "I thought your grandfather said he'd clean all this while I was out."

"Gramps took out his hearing aids and went upstairs right after you left." I look at the empty cake plate. "I was going to clean my mess up, but then, you know." I point to the crate.

She sighs, and bangs on the broken soap dispenser. "I'm sorry that Cal put you in that crate, Stanley. It was a terrible trick. I'll punish him, to be sure. But I have to say it: I'm a little worried about you, kiddo. I wish you'd learn to stand up for yourself more."

I can't believe my ears. "Stand up for myself more? Nice, Mom. Blame the victim, why don't you."

Mom's eyes narrow. "Watch your tone, Stan."

"Mom, Cal's got thirty pounds on me. I've been the smallest kid in every class I've ever been in. And now that I'm in middle school, I'm the smallest kid in the whole place. It's not a matter of standing up for myself. It's a matter of physics. Weight. Mass. Force. POWER. Other kids have it. I don't."

I stare at the floor. It's covered in chocolate cake crumbs.

"Oh, honey." Mom reaches out and strokes my forehead with her soapy, damp hand, like she's trying to wipe my feelings away. "I know the new school's hard. I know you don't like it. But . . . maybe if you tried just a little harder. Talk to the other kids. Why don't you ever talk to anyone?"

I shake my head. I'm not a talker. I don't say much, unless it's Mom, Dad, Gramps, or Joon. My Safe People.

"I know! Why don't you join one of the after-school clubs?"

My stomach squirms. "There are no good ones."

"So start your own! No one knows more about comics than you—why don't you start a comic book club?"

Yeah, great. She might as well be asking me to start a Let's Beat Up Stanley Club.

"Well, you need to do something," Mom says. "You hardly leave your room. You need more social interaction. Where's your old buddy Joon these days? Why's he never around?"

My stomach contracts into a squirmy ball. "Dunno," I say, my voice tight. "He's around."

"Hey, I've got an idea."

Uh-oh.

"What about that new girl next door?" Mom side-eyes me. "I hear she's homeschooled. It must be lonely for her; I bet she'd just love to make a nice new friend like you! I met the uncle by the mailbox the other day. Dr. Silverberg. It's just the two of them; her mom's living somewhere else for a while. But anyway, he seems very nice."

"You think everyone is nice."

"Well, most people are." She gives me an encouraging smile. "If you give them a chance. And this niece could be nice, too. She's your age. New in town. Doesn't know a soul." Mom turns off the tap and dries her hands. Then she gives me The Look again. "I mean it, Stanley. I want you to start speaking to other kids. I want you to go over there and welcome that new girl to the neighborhood. It's an assignment. No: a command. You're going over there tomorrow, and that's final."

What can I do? I know defeat when I see it.

After we finish cleaning the kitchen, I trudge up to my room. I shut the door tight, sprawl on my bed, and stare at my wall.

We moved here when I was four, right after Mom and Dad got their Friendly Divorce. Back then, I loved rocket ships and outer space, so Mom spent a week painting planets all over my walls. She meant well, but to be honest, she's no Michelangelo. Everything's kind of blotchy. Saturn's rings pretty much look ready to wobble right out of the galaxy.

Still, Mom tries. She works really, really hard—as a real estate broker and as a tax accountant. And ever since Gramps moved in with us over the summer, Mom looks even more tired than usual.

My dad used to come over a lot, to help with house projects, and homework, and just to be with me and Cal. But now he works for this global charity, building clinics and schools in Africa. It's his dream job. But I don't like him being gone.

My dad's French, but born in Morocco, which is in northern Africa. That's why our last name is Fortinbras—it sort of means "strong arms" in French. My dad has strong arms. He's small, strong, dark, and handsome, and he's really, really good at helping other people.

He used to be good at helping us.

I, on the other hand, do not have strong arms. My arms are basically two overcooked pieces of spaghetti.

Anyhow. When I worry about stuff—like Dad being gone, or Calvin turning Hulk, or Joon drifting away—I like to hole up in my room. It's a pretty okay place, despite Mom's wacky space mural. I've got a super-tall stack of comics by my desk, and superhero posters, and a new drafting table for sketching and cartooning. The bed's comfy, and I'm at the end of the hall, so it's quiet. Quiet is of primo importance to me. I can't handle too much noise, or craziness, or stress. I get what Mom calls sensory overload.

Between the new school and home lately, there's a lot of sensory overload.

In fact, more and more, I'm starting to feel like

this room is the only calm place I've got left in the whole universe.

Even if it's a universe where all the planets are a little out of whack.

3

MONDAY MORNING, 6:50 alarm. I open my eyes and think: five whole miserable days at Peavey Middle School stretch in front of me. Ugh.

Plus today's the day Mom's forcing me to go say hello to that new girl next door. Double ugh.

I hit snooze and drift . . . until my eyes fly open in a panic. It's 7:05!

Red Alert!

Red Alert!

Pretend your body's the starship *Enterprise*, and it's going into emergency mode: woop woop. With each woop, liquid panic pulses from your guts to the tips of your fingers and toes.

Lots of things give me Red Alerts. Principal Coffin's safety drills. Fear of crowds. Too much noise. Getting stuck in a dog crate.

Missing the school bus!

I throw my clothes on and pound downstairs in record time. Whew! Cal's still in the kitchen, cramming papers in his backpack while shoveling toast in his face. But it's 7:09, and at 7:09, I know for a fact the bus is already on Canyon Rim.

"Come on!" I say, jumping up and down to help ease the panging Red Alert panic. "We're going to miss it!"

Cal opens wide to show me his mouthful of disgusting mush. "Go by yourself, dweeb."

"Mom says we're supposed to go together!" I say. Which is true. It's also true that the six-lane intersection on Canyon Rim, with its honking cars and bus exhaust, freaks me out just enough that I'd rather wait for Cal.

We run-walk down our drive, then past the neighbors. That new girl is probably still in bed. Homeschooled. She can probably do whatever the heck she wants today. No Peavey Middle School of Panic. What the heck does Mom want me to say to her? Just ring the bell and—what then? Why does Mom like to torture me with requests like this? Glurgh. My stomach tightens.

Cal and I jog up the hill, each road and intersection

getting busier and busier. At the traffic light, our bus is a flash of yellow, just pulling away! But Cal, who's a fast sprinter, takes off and waves it down.

The doors hiss open, and Olga points a blue-nailed finger at us, from up on the driver's seat. "That's two times in one month for you boys. I'm not putting up with any more what you call lollygagging," she says in her Russian accent.

Cal grunts and pushes past.

"He's sorry, Olga. I'm sorry," I whisper, gasping, my heart pounding from the run. "It won't happen again."

Olga's always got a trucker's cap on, a big wad of gum in her mouth, and mirrored wraparound sunglasses. I've never seen her eyes. She keeps the local radio station turned up so loud on her bus, my head pounds. And it seems like every other song is by this band named Blue Paloma that the girls are nuts about. They usually sit in the front seats by the speaker, singing louder and louder until Olga shouts, "Hey, pop divas, simmer down!"

The bus lurches forward, and I practically fall into my usual seat next to Joon.

"Dude." Joon fist-bumps me as the bus heads out. "Guess what? My oldest sister Kari got a nose ring and shaved her head. Mom was so mad she was shouting in

14

Korean so fast no one could tell what she was saying." Joon touches his own thick brown hair. Lately, he's started spiking it into pointy triangles with a ton of this stinky gel. I haven't said anything to him yet, but I think Joon's probably been watching too much *Dragon Ball Z*.

"Maybe you should just shave it all off, too," I suggest. "The Green Lama's bald, right?"

He gives me a dirty look.

I don't know why because Joon's always loved the Green Lama. It's been his favorite vintage comic superhero since fourth grade. A superpowered Buddhist monk from the 1940s who fights evil in a glowing green cloak? What's not to like? "The Lama puts the om in O-M-G!" Joon used to say to me. "Never diss the Lama!"

We ride a while in silence. Then I take a breath and ask him something I never used to have to ask, because it was a given: "So . . . do you want to hang out together this weekend?"

Joon doesn't answer right away. He's staring at Gaby Garcia, two seats up. Joon would submit to torture before actually admitting he likes Gaby, but I can tell he does.

"Well . . . I was thinking about biking to the comic shop on Saturday," Joon says. "Like I've told you, I'm kind of over just hanging at our houses."

The only time Joon ever talked me into biking to the

15

comic shop was last year. My pant leg got caught in the chain, and I had to stop for him to fix it for me. Then, the busy traffic and noise of Camino Real spooked me so much, I skidded through a bunch of gears by accident, wiped out, and almost got hit by a car. I'm not what you'd call a cycling enthusiast.

"If you hang at my house this weekend instead of biking," I say, "I'll give you one of my comics—you don't need to buy one."

He shakes his head so that the gel-spikes tremble. "Dude," Joon says, looking kind of sad. "We should do stuff."

I frown. "I do stuff."

"No, you don't."

"I went to the town pool with you a few weeks ago."

"And you stood around in the shallow end with a bunch of ninety-year-old men. It was embarrassing."

"I don't like to swim in the deep end. Plus those guys were interesting."

"Dude. Half the girls in the seventh grade were there. That was interesting."

I look at the hair-flippers in the front seat, shrieking along to the radio, and cover my ears. Joon sinks down in his seat, looking gloomy.

Finally, the bus pulls into the school drive. And at

the same time, Olga's radio goes:

GLONNGGGG!!

Blue Paloma cuts out, and a smooth, deep voice comes on instead. It's kind of a cross between Severus Snape and a monster-truck announcer.

"Greetings, comics fans! Some call me the greatest comic artist of all time. But what is time? Time, dear fans, is fluid, more fluid than the ink with which I draw and create my Galaktikan-Metropole worlds."

Joon and I snap to attention.

"Whoa," Joon says. "Is that—it can't be—is that—"

"It is! It's the Master!" I say, feeling giddy. One of the biggest names in comics is speaking to us on the radio! He's got movies, graphic novels, you name it. He's got his own TV show. Big stuff. We stare at each other in disbelief.

"Comic Fest is coming soon, and to celebrate, I'm announcing something new this year: Trivia Quest! A giant trivia treasure hunt that will take place all around downtown San Diego! Enter Trivia Quest, solve all the clues, and you will receive a super VIP behind-the-scenes pass for the following weekend to . . . Comic Fest!!"

Win a pass to Comic Fest? That's the biggest comics convention in the country. Cool costumes! Famous people! Fan gear and gizmos! I follow it online and on

TV every year, like gazillions of others. But the odds of scoring tickets are about the same as getting bitten by a mutant spider and turned into Spider-Man.

"Finish the Quest," says the Master on the radio, "And get into the Fest! And what's more—"

Olga snaps the radio off. "Outta here, lollygaggers," she yells.

"Dude!" Joon's eyes are barely focusing. He points a trembling finger at the radio. "That . . . Trivia Quest thing? We. Are. So. Doing. That!" Then he puts up both fists for a bump.

I nod and smile. Blood is beginning to pound in my ears. I almost can't breathe, I'm so excited. Because no one knows comic book trivia like I do. It's my one and only superpower. This Trivia Quest thing is made for someone like me to enter! And Joon knows it!

For once, he'll totally need me!

But . . . But . . .

Wait.

The Quest is all the way downtown. It sounds hard. And crowded. And long. And exhausting. And noisy. And . . .

Joon is 100 percent pumped.

"YES!" I say, fist-bumping him. "We are SO doing that!"

My stomach's a little queasy, but I can overlook it.

18

Because as we're leaving the bus, Joon kind of jumps on my back and punches me on my shoulder, and then he grins at me like the Joon I used to know. The Joon who used to be proud to be my friend.

4

PEOPLE, PEOPLE!

Once we're inside, we see Mrs. Green standing in the middle of the sixth-grade hall and clapping like she's trying to scatter pigeons. "Get what you need from your lockers and head right down to the auditorium for a surprise assembly!"

Nooo! Not again!

As if on cue, Principal Coffin's voice booms and crackles out of the speakers. "It's Monday morning, and it's Tiiiime for Safety!"

Principal Coffin throws these extreme-edition assemblies and drills all the time, and the whole middle school is forced to go. We never know when they're going to happen. She likes to keep us guessing.

Rumor has it that some hideous catastrophe happened at her old school, and they were totally unprepared. So now it's her personal mission to prepare us. Earthquake, fire, tsunami, flood, blackout, gas leak, first aid, CPR, stranger danger, bomb threat: you name it, we've drilled it at Peavey Middle School of Panic. I mean, being prepared is important, but Principal Coffin is over-the-top gonzo.

When I get to the auditorium, Joon's nowhere in sight, and of course I end up stuck in the back row next to Kyle Keefner.

"Get away from me, Fart-in-bra," he barks.

Kyle Keefner hates me. He decided to hate me back in kindergarten, and it's been that way ever since. Joon figures Kyle will finally beat me up someday, and it'll be over. But I think Keefner enjoys hating me too much for it ever to be over.

Up on stage, Principal Coffin's talking with two firefighters. She's a big plump lady with grizzled gray hair and a booming voice. She's usually nice—but don't get her angry, or she'll go full-scale Hulk on you. At least, that's what Cal says. Me, I'm too scared of getting in trouble to ever get in trouble.

Right now she taps the microphone, and I cover my ears. "Take your seats, darlins!" she says. "We have potentially lifesaving information this morning so we need everyone's attention immediately. I'm serious, chickens. This info could mean Life. Or. Death."

Why does she have to say life or death all the time? Also, why does she call us chickens? We keep chickens at home—we have a coop with eight hens behind the house. Chickens are all right, but you should smell their poop. Ugh.

"Let me introduce these hometown heroes," she says, pointing at the firefighters. "These brave folks have seen children just like you perish in fires. Terrible, painful tragedies. And why?" Principal Coffin cocks her ear to hear our answer. "WHY do people die horribly in fires?" Behind her on the projection screen, photos of burning homes flash.

I can already imagine flames leaping around my feet.

"What do I always tell you we need to be?"

"Prepared!" someone shouts from the front row.

"That's right, my adorable, plucky little chickens!" Principal Coffin beams out at us. "Because they were not prepared. But we are not going to let that happen to anyone in Peavey Middle School! Peavey is PREPARED! Say it with me!"

Mrs. Coffin raises both arms up, casting a giant, evil-looking shadow on the burning-inferno screen behind her. "Peavey is safe! Peavey is prepared! Say it with me, people!"

A few kids mumble it.

"Now I need a volunteer to come up on stage," calls Principal Coffin, shading her eyes with her hand and peering out at us. "To help in a little demonstration. How about one of you boys? In the back row, sticking out of the aisle, there, who's that?"

Oh no—

"Is that Stanley, I see? Little Stanley Fortinbras, come on up here, Stanley!"

Kyle Keefner is shaking with glee. "Go on, little Stanley Fart-in-bra!" he snorts, giving me a shove.

Kids turn and stare. My stomach clenches. My heart rabbit-thumps against my ribs.

Red Alert!

Red Alert!

But there's no way out. I hear deafening claps and cheering as I wobble forward in a daze. Kids' hands reach out into the aisle to push me along, or try to slap me five. Why are they acting like I'm the lucky one or something? This is not a good thing! I—I can't see—as usual, my glasses are smudged so everything looks foggy.

Principal Coffin's hand reaches down and pulls me up the steps. Before I know it, I'm standing under the stage lights. A firefighter slams a hat on my head, and another puts me in a giant coat that weighs a ton.

23

Sensory alert! Sensory alert!

They hand me a stick of some sort. Everything's muffled, like I'm in a dream. The lights and sounds have me in a sort of state of shock. Is that roar I hear coming from out in the audience, or from inside my own brain?

"Okay, kiddo, we're gonna demo this here super-fast extinguisher. We'll set that torch you're holding on fire," the first firefighter says into her microphone, looming toward me with a big red canister. "And then we're gonna put you out! Fun, right?"

Wait—did she say "put it out" or "put me out"? Suddenly I have a gross metal tang in my mouth. The back of my throat is dry, and my hands feel tingly. All the faces out there in the dark, watching me, watching! Noise! Lights! Heavy coat! Heat! Can't see! World is blurry! Are they planning to set me on fire? Has everyone at Peavey gone insane? Why, oh why can't I be homeschooled like that new neighbor girl, what's her name?

My knees feel funny.

Woop! Woop!

My vision starts fading, turning black at the edges . . . My legs are Jell-O. . . .

Somewhere in a distant fog I think I hear Kyle Keefner shout: "Hey, cool, look! Fart-in-bra's fainting! He's goin' down!"

5

THEY DRAG ME backstage onto a metal folding chair that's stuck in the folds of a giant, dusty black curtain. I immediately start sneezing.

Principal Coffin and a firefighter are bent over me. Their voices buzz and catch in the curtain folds. What are they saying?

They help me stand, slowly. "Easy, now, kiddo," someone says. Then they help me totter out the stage door and into the brightness of the main hall where a custodian is waiting with a walkie-talkie; he keeps hold of my arm as we walk to the main office. I keep my head down, staring at floor tiles in total humiliation. At least I didn't have to do a walk of shame past the kids in the auditorium.

It's starting to sink in, what just happened. I just fainted in front of the entire population of Peavey Middle School.

I'm doomed.

In the office, a tall lady with dark brown skin smiles kindly down at me. She's wearing a purple Peavey tracksuit with a name badge that reads *Mrs. Ngozo, Guidance Counselor.* "Thank you, Doc," she says to the custodian. "You may go." She ushers me into the health room, and forces me to lie down on this disgusting, fleshy-pink leather sickbed they've got in there.

She puts a cold cloth on my head and shoves a thermometer in my ear. I'm so nervous, from the stage, the fainting, and now the couch, that I'm still kind of panting. So she gets this paper bag and puts it in front of my face. It smells like someone's tuna fish sandwich and banana just got dumped out of it. "Breathe, Stanley, breathe!" she urges.

Then Mrs. Ngozo does something even worse: she calls my mom. I can hear them talking in the next room. "I see. The poor boy," I hear Mrs. Ngozo say. "Tsk tsk. Uh-huh. I do agree . . . anxiety . . . sensory issues . . . need to support . . . suppose we could consider . . . yes."

When she comes back in, I'm sitting up. I've pushed down all the stress, all the worry, everything I've been feeling. I've swallowed it, and I've put a fake smile on my face instead. I've got to get out of here.

"I'm great, now, Mrs. Ngozo," I whisper in a small, dry voice. My heart's still pounding, and I'm sweating in all kinds of new places. But I just want the day to go back to normal. I want to be like those ice-skaters you see on TV who fall, then get up so fast and continue on, you barely register that they even fell. Maybe if I get back to class quick, kids will think it was no big deal.

Mrs. Ngozo perches on the edge of a chair near me. Her perfume is so strong I have to inch back toward the wall and hold my breath. I distract myself from the aroma-onslaught by staring at the tiny brown braids that loop and twist like a crown on the top of her head.

"You're shaking, young man. I can practically see the stress coming off you in waves. Okay, put away that paper bag; I will teach you a better self-calming technique. Think of a color you like. A soothing color."

I sigh. For some reason, Aquaman pops into my mind. "Aqua?" I whisper, to humor her.

"And what's a color that you hate, Stanley?"

I once found this Crayola crayon the exact color of chicken poop. "Ochre."

"I want you to do a little exercise. Breathe in good thoughts and good air, thinking about aqua. Then slowly expel your bad thoughts and bad air, thinking ochre."

It's weird, but better than the stinky paper bag.

"Excellent," she says. "See? Now you're breathing calmly. And so, let's talk. Your mother is wondering if our Peavey safety assemblies might be rather too, er, intense for you." She gives me a Mom-style, soul-searing look.

I shrug. The lump in my throat gets bigger.

"Your mother informed me, confidentially, that you have sensory processing disorder. Things seem too loud, too strong, too bright, too tight, too much . . . Too much noise, too many crowds, these types of things are hard for you, yes?" There's that look again. Ouch.

Why would Mom tell her about that? I don't like anyone to know.

"Don't worry. I won't mention it to anyone. But here's the thing . . . your mother thought perhaps we could find a quiet zone for you here at school, somewhere safe, for when things get to be too much. What do you think?"

I shrug again. Although my brain is still buzzing, the thought of no noise, no craziness, is nice. Just a few peaceful minutes. Then I'll be fine. "Okay," I mumble. I feel miserable. And like all my energy is gone.

Mrs. Ngozo smiles, and leads me out to a beige-carpeted back hallway. Just past an office with her name, there's an unmarked door. She turns the knob, and clicks on the switch.

A desk, a chair, empty gray bookshelves, and one of those big meeting-presentation-type easels with a giant sketchpad on it. That's all that's in there.

"What if you were able to come here whenever you're feeling overwhelmed? It's quiet. You can bring your schoolwork. It's safe. And if you feel as if you want to talk to me, my office is right here. We don't want to cause you to feel faint again! Do you think this could be helpful to you, Stanley?"

I feel like an idiot. But I nod.

"Then I'll fill your teachers in. And remember: aqua and ochre!" She closes the door gently.

I slump into the desk chair and put my head in my arms. I'm not going to cry or anything. I'm just sick and tired of being in this stupid new school. Why can't I be homeschooled, like that neighbor kid? Why can't I just be home, right now, where it's safe?

I can still faintly hear the chaos of that assembly through the open intercom channel down the hall. There's music blaring—burn baby burn, disco inferno!—and kids are clapping and screaming as Principal Coffin's voice booms out like a commando of doom: "Stop, drop, and roll! Stop, drop, and roll!"

I sigh. So what do I do? I could review my homework that's due today, but I already know I got everything right. I always get everything right. I never make a big deal about it, but it's another reason why Kyle Keefner hates me.

I poke around in the desk drawers. They're pretty empty—except for half a pink eraser, a bunch of old staples, and in the big bottom drawer, some big boxes of markers. I take a black one out, uncap it, and inhale the sharp tang of the wedged felt-tip. Then I look over at that giant sketchpad, standing on the easel in the corner.

It's open to a new white page. Funny. I could have sworn that pad was closed a few seconds ago. I bring a box of markers over to the easel, and touch the black marker tip to the blank page, and do what I always do when I can't think straight or when my heart feels weird and heavy.

I draw.

I draw me wearing that heavy fire coat, curled up in Albert Einstein's dog crate, while flames surround me, closer, and closer, under a big sign that says *Peavey Middle School of Panic*, and I write, in the speech bubble: HELP! GET ME OUT OF HERE!

At lunch a few hours later, I sit in a free spot by Joon. Across from us is Dylan Bustamante, Keefner, and some kids from 6-G and 6-S I've never talked to. Actually, most of the kids from 6-G and 6-S are kids I've never talked to.

"You were late to math this morning. What happened on stage?" Joon asks.

"You were all slumped over," says Dylan Bustamante. "Did you faint for real?"

"I bet it was an act," Joon says, covering for me so I don't have to answer. "But, hey, hey, do you guys think we're really going to dissect worms in science today?"

I flash him a look of relief, but he's not looking at me.

They start talking science and worms and what the inside of a worm looks like, and everything's okay. I'm off the hook, and the worm's on.

When lunch is over, I try to walk out with Joon, saying, "Hey, thanks—"

But he skips ahead with the others, like all of a sudden he's mad at me or something.

See, this is why I don't talk to people. I have no idea what's going on them half the time.

6

THAT AFTERNOON, I walk home from the bus stop full of worry because now I'm supposed to go ring the doorbell of that new neighbor girl.

It never works out when your mom forces you to be friends with someone. In second grade, my mom did PTO stuff with Kyle Kecfner's mom, and made me come along so I could play with Kyle. They'd have coffee in the kitchen while Kyle pinned me to the floor of the playroom and stuffed the yellow heads of mini LEGO people up my nostrils. "See? Didn't I tell you it'd be fun?" she'd say on the way home. Yeah. Thanks, Mom.

But I did promise to obey Mom's command to go say hi to this girl. So I stop at the curb in front of her house to try to get up enough courage to go ring the bell, get the whole thing over with . . . when I see something weird.

There's this giant pine tree that grows between our driveway and theirs. And all the way up near the top its branches are rustling. I see a flash of bright red.

At first I imagine some kind of weird parrot or something. But then there's a human arm, in a red T-shirt, grabbing for a branch. Then two dirty purple sneakers, scrambling by the trunk.

What do I do? Shout "Hello, welcome to the neighborhood" up the tree, where she's dangling, now? What if I startle her and make her lose her balance?

Better just tiptoe past.

I'm just about to do that when she shouts, "Who's down there?"

I clear my throat a couple of times, then call up into the branches, my voice all croaking and weird: "You should probably try not to fall. Also, my mom told me to say hello to you."

I cringe. Was that okay?

Nothing from her. No response.

Just as I'm turning to go, and feeling really stupid, the voice calls back. "I'm not falling. And why do you care what your mom tells you?" The purple sneakers and stork legs struggle even higher, up into the very topmost branches.

34

She's climbing way too high. My heart pounds. "Hey, seriously. You could fall! What are you trying to prove?"

The whole top of the tree is bending and swaying now. One purple-sneakered foot flails off a branch then scrambles back on.

I hold my breath as her hand reaches out and touches the tiptop branch. There's a whoop of glee. "I see it!" she shouts.

"See what?" I shout back.

A face appears, up high between the branches, pale, but beaming. "The ocean! I see it!"

"Just . . . don't fall!" I turn to go. "Oh—and welcome to the neighborhood!" I add, in a way that probably doesn't sound too welcoming.

I can't watch this. If she goes splat, she goes splat.

Back in my room, I pass the time until dinner by flipping through a stack of vintage Weird Mysteries comics. And I try not to look out my window at that pine tree. In fact, I close the curtain.

Mom's late—big surprise—and Gramps is at the kitchen table, reading the business section and rubbing stinky ointment into his bum shoulder. He's always either at that table reading the news, or in his recliner watching weird TV shows, and grumbling the whole time. Gramps has had some money and health troubles. He had to sell his farm last year and move in with us, and he can get pretty grumpy.

It's hard for Gramps to do a lot of things now—including dinner prep, because he has Parkinson's and his hands are starting to shake. He says the only food prep he's good at is salting or peppering things.

Because Calvin usually has sports practice after school, and Mom's always working, and Gramps's hands shake, dinner prep usually means me. I set the table around the newspaper, pull out a frozen lasagna, stick it in the oven, and wash some lettuce. Then I go outside and feed the chickens.

I glance over my shoulder, back up the drive—there's no sign of a splatted human under the pine tree, so that's good. If I were homeschooled, the last thing I'd do is risk my life climbing up a tree just to stare at the ocean. I'd be in my room, having fun, reading comics. But, instead, I have to go to a big prison of a middle school. And make dinner. And do a million chores. And put up with Gramps. And Cal.

Mom gets home late, and she's so pooped from all the real-estating and accounting, she doesn't even notice we're eating lasagna that's frozen in the middle. Calvin scoops all the good melted-cheese bits from around the edges. Then he says with an evil grin, "Hey, Mom.

Stannie got called up on stage at assembly this morning in front of everyone, and he totally lost it."

"Hush!" Mom cuts him off. "I know all about that already. Leave your poor little brother alone."

Cal scowls, and shovels in some more lasagna. I don't say anything, but I hate being the "poor little brother."

The rest of the meal, Gramps grumbles about how he should've bought this stock, or could have bought that property until Mom says, "Okay, Dad, enough complaining." She points at him with her fork. "It's too stressful to think that way. I'm reading this wonderful book about being more mindful in the moment. It's called *No More Woulda-Shoulda-Coulda.*" She looks around at all of us, smiling. "Pay attention, Stanley. This might be helpful to you about lowering your anxiety. The book says to practice mindful living. Notice every moment. Live in the present tense, enjoying the beauty of the here and now. It's a very Buddhist-like philosophy. Isn't it beautiful? No more woulda-shoulda-coulda."

Cal snorts. "Yeah, like you live in the moment. You live in the office!"

Mom's smile droops. "You have a point there, bucko," she says.

Gramps takes another sip of his beer and shakes his head. "Shoulda been a Buddhist," he says.

After cleanup, we all move to the TV room. Gramps

grumps at the news anchor from his recliner while Mom works on her laptop. I'm doing math homework, with Albert Einstein curled up on top of my feet. Calvin's on the couch, chucking a football up in the air, over and over.

"So help me, if you smash something . . . ," Mom murmurs from behind her laptop screen. But Cal just keeps whipping the ball at the ceiling.

"Breaking news from Uganda," says some lady on the TV news, a hand on her earpiece.

And we all freeze.

When my dad first started this new travel job, Mom had taped a giant paper world map on the living room wall for Cal and me so we could track him. Red pins show all the places Dad's been, on his "midlife crisis mission to save the world," as Mom calls it. And one single green pin marks where he is now. The map's totally pockmarked with red pins.

"This just in," the TV person says. "A massive explosion near government buildings in Kampala has resulted in evacuations, and early reports of casualties are coming in . . ."

Nobody moves. The football stays in Cal's hands. Then all four of our heads swivel simultaneously to look at that world map. All of our eyes focus on the location of the one, small, green, pin.

Mom's eyes widen, then she starts typing furiously on her laptop. "Just wait a minute. Let me call up your father's latest schedule. Wait. Wait."

Red Alert.

Red Alert.

On the television the smoke is still billowing from the airport in Kampala. Mom is still tapping furiously on her laptop and jabbing at the buttons on her phone. "Wait!" she says. "I've texted him. Wait!"

So we wait. I rub my clammy hands on the knees of my jeans and try to calm down. My eyes are riveted onto the news.

On the screen, the black billowing smoke footage has changed to a scene of ambulances and police across the street, and dirty, dazed people milling about. Some type of scuffle and screaming breaks out behind an on-the-scenes reporter.

"Principal Coffin would say they need to file out of there quickly and orderly," says Cal, clutching the football tightly, his voice low and quiet.

Woop, goes my stomach. Woop.

Tap tap, go Mom's fingers, flying on her laptop.

"Wait!" Mom finally shouts. "He's not even in Kampala right now . . ." She exhales a gush of air. "He left there . . . two weeks ago!?" She rubs her eyes; they look bloodshot and bleary. "I totally forgot about moving that stupid pin!"

We all let out a whoosh of air we didn't realize we'd been holding.

That's how long my Dad's been away from us. So long that he could be anywhere on that big stupid wall map. So long that we've stopped remembering to even keep track.

7

THE REST OF the school week is pretty much okay. All Joon wants to talk about on the bus is the Trivia Quest, which makes me nervous. But on the plus side, Principal Coffin doesn't hold any more safety assemblies.

I also haven't been sleeping well all this week. My mind's too full of fire drills and airport explosions and purple sneakers flailing in the tops of trees.

So Saturday morning, when the phone rings early, I'm groggy.

"Hey. So I'm thinking Trivia Quest!" Joon says. "Let's make a plan. You want to bring a stack of your comics over?"

My eyes snap open. He wants to hang out? It's been eons since I spent a Saturday at Joon's. We used to, all the time. But he's been so busy, with soccer and every-thing.

"Five minutes," I tell him, grinning, "I'm there."

As I head out, I glance next door. I haven't seen the neighbor girl since Monday. I told Mom I did my duty and said hello, and left it at that.

But now, when I get to the end of the drive, there she is, by the garbage pails, flattening out a bunch of card-board moving boxes.

I freeze. She looks different, up close and out of the tree.

She must be at least six feet tall, taller than Calvin, and skinny. Like, bony-skinny. Her hair's bleached white, and shorter than mine. Below her forehead, she's got kind of watery, green, bulging eyes

Along with ripped black leggings, she's got on a giant, dress-sized sweatshirt that says *Frolicking Kittens*.

"It's a band," she says to me.

"What?"

"Frolicking Kittens. That's what you're looking at, right?" She drops the piece of flattened cardboard she was holding, and pulls the sweatshirt out by the corners to better show off the picture of kittens. They have red fangs, and blood dripping from their claws. "It's my mom's old boyfriend's band."

"Okay. Cool." My heart's hammering, like it always does when I talk to a new person. I try to stare up at her face, not her shirt. At her watery, too-wide eyes.

"When I was really little, we traveled around with them on tour," she says. "But they broke up. Not the band—my mom and the drummer. And all I got was this lousy T-shirt." She grins. Her teeth are small, with spaces between them.

"So," I hear myself say. "W-where'd you move from?"

"Pittsburgh, the last couple of years, living with my uncle and my mom. Then my uncle moved here, and my mom and I figured we'd come, too—but she's in LA, to try acting, and so, well, I decided to come here, to . . ." She gets a cloudy look on her face.

"To what?"

She shrugs. "Nothing. To keep Uncle Dan company, and help him with the move." She puts her words in air quotes.

I have no idea what she's talking about, so I just stare at her shoes.

"Liberty," she finally says.

"And justice for all?" I say.

"No, stupid." She snort-laughs. "That's my name."

"Okay." I swallow, hard.

"How old are you?" She nudges my shoulder with her

bony elbow, and I take a step back.

"Almost thirteen," I say. "Technically, twelve and nine months."

Her eyebrows raise. "Wow. I'm less than a year older than you, and seriously about twice your height." She snort-laughs again. "We're extremes, all right."

I scuff one sneaker against the other and steal a glance up the road where Joon's waiting. "Yeah, I guess. I mean, you're right. I'm the smallest kid in school. But extremes are no good. I'd rather be the norm."

"Okay, then." She puts out her hand. "Nice to meet you, Norm."

I shake her hand quickly. Then I sprint up the road. I'm sweating and all stressed out.

At the corner, I look back, and Liberty Silverberg is still standing there, watching me. She looks like an Axi-Tun warrior. A member of that alien race from the Fantastic Four. The Axi-Tun were giants, with the super-power of being able to manipulate energy.

Which makes sense. Because I feel like I just escaped from some kind of freakish force field.

Joon's mom opens the door before I can knock, and stops yelling into her phone just long enough to shove a napkin with some home-baked protein bars into my hands. They're crispy-chewy-salty and pretty much one of my favorite foods.

"Very healthy! Full of protein. Eat 'em and like 'em," she orders. "Complaint department, fifth floor."

That's our standard joke because there's no fifth floor at Joon's.

Joon says his mom is the most uptight yoga studio owner in existence, but I like that you always know where you stand with Mrs. Lee because she will tell you flat out. There's something calming about that.

Joon's upstairs, lying on his bed in a pile of comics and dirty laundry. I offer him a protein bar, but he waves it away.

"You're in, for sure? No scaredy-cat backing out? We're doing the Trivia Quest, definitely, right?" Joon flaps one of his silly Captain Carrot and the Zoo Crew comics in my face.

"For sure!" I say. "Me? Back out?" I laugh. Ha ha! What an absolutely ridiculous question.

"Trivia Quest is a big deal, Stan. There's tons of teams already signed up. I've checked everything out online. Seven clues. One day. And the clues can be about any-thing—any comic, from any time period. So I need you. Don't wig out on me."

"No problema!" I say, all fake-cheerful, even though

my brain's already flashing with possible disaster scenarios. Maybe getting down to work will help. I open my backpack. "Okay. Here. I made some comic history charts last week in study hall, just in case. Let's start with the Golden Age of Comics, 1930s to 1950s." I smooth out the folds in my pieces of paper, stare at my small, careful lettering. Just looking at the charts calms and comforts me. This is order. This is control. If I concentrate just on the trivia, and I don't think about the Quest itself, I just might get through it.

"How about we go through the superheroes one by one," I say.

Joon grabs the chart from me. "Hey, there's the Green Lama! Whoa. How many names on this list?"

"A ton of superheroes were born during the Golden Age. Superman, Batman, Robin, Wonder Woman, the Flash, Green Lantern, the Atom, Hawkman, Green Arrow, and Aquaman . . . And that's just on the DC side. Now, Marvel, or what was going to turn into Marvel, they created the Human Torch, Sub-Mariner, Captain America . . ."

"Captain Marvel," Joon adds.

"Er, no."

He squints. "Captain Marvel is not Marvel Comics?"

"He was under Fawcett. Then DC bought Fawcett."

46

"So Captain Marvel is a DC comic? That's weird."

"Well, yeah. Sorta. And then, the comic got renamed Shazam. And later, there was this thing called the Crisis on Infinite Earths, which led to a bunch of reboots, when a lot of stuff changed around. You'll see—"

That's when Joon gets a glazed look and says he has to go to the bathroom. While he's gone my thoughts slide back to the contest. I go to the official website on his laptop, just to see what I'm getting myself into.

At Trivia Quest, hundreds of comics fans from all over the world will compete for clues that send them to many local landmarks all around scenic downtown San Diego. For every clue solved, one gold token is awarded. Contestants who solve seven clues and collect seven gold tokens will automatically be awarded VIP passes to Comic Fest, which starts the following weekend! But never fear—there are consolation prizes as well. . . .

Hmm. Sounds intimidating.

"Joon," I say as he comes back in. "You know, Trivia Quest sounds pretty much mainly for superfans. And grown-ups. This has to be only for grown-ups."

"Nope. Read on, dude."

I skim down the fine print and sure enough: "Ages twelve to eighteen welcome to register with signed permission from a parent or guardian . . ."

My stomach flops. How will I handle a whole day in a crowd downtown?

"It's gonna be awesome!" Joon shouts.

I try to smile. "Yeah! Awesome!" I say, slapping him five.

I pray he doesn't notice how weak my high five is.

8

COMING BACK HOME from Joon's, I open our front door—
and there's Cal, fist-pumping and leaping around the
living room like a maniac.

"YES!"

He's about to knock over a floor lamp.

"YES YES YESSS!"

"NO!" Mom says, diving for the lamp with one hand
and swiping for the long, thin package Cal's holding
with the other. "I swear I'm going to shoot your grandfather! In a manner of speaking."

"What's going on here?" I say.

"Gramps gave me the hunting rifle I wanted for my
birthday!" Cal shouts joyfully. "A .22!"

Gramps comes shuffling in from the kitchen,

clutching his cane in one hand and a coffee cup in the other. "Darn straight I did," he says. "The boy's fourteen, Jane! Ain't nothing wrong with it!" He glares at Mom from under his wiry gray eyebrows. "Let the boy grow up! Cal's more than old enough. Hell, even Stanley here's old enough for target practice. OOH-yah." Gramps ends a lot of sentences with "OOH-yah," because he's from what he calls "dang near indestructible Norwegian farm stock."

"Target practice where? We don't have forty acres of cornfields out back, like you did, Dad," Mom says, shaking her head and frowning.

Gramps really misses his cornfields. And hunting. He loves going on about it and about how great life was back in the simpler time of the early Pleistocene, or whenever it was he grew up. The menfolk would go deer hunting every November, ice fishing every February . . .

But Mom says she never did understand killing things for pleasure. Anyway, right now Mom is yelling, and Gramps is yelling, and Cal is aiming the rifle out the window at Dr. Silverberg, Liberty's uncle, who's innocently headed to his mailbox.

Mom swipes the gun from Cal's hands. "End of story. I'm locking it away right now."

"But—I'm fourteen!"

"Not another word!"

Cal's face is flushed. "Well . . . who else is going to man up around here?" he bellows.

Mom wrinkles her nose and jolts her head back. "What on earth are you talking about?"

"Who's gonna protect us?" Cal's fuming. "You're always working. Dad's ditched us. Gramps is too old. Who's the man in charge?"

Mom's eyes bulge, and she starts rumbling like she's a volcano about to erupt. "Who on earth in this day and age says there has to be a man in charge, Calvin Fortinbras? I'm working two jobs, running this house, feeding you, clothing you, doing everything around here—and there has to be a man in charge? What on God's green earth do you think we need protecting from? Has Gramps got you thinking you're Daniel Boone, living in the wild frontier, with all this gun nonsense?"

I feel like I should do or say something. But I don't know what. So I just stand there, frozen, clutching at my backpack. Wanting everyone to stop shouting.

Sensory alert.

"What about the coyotes?" Cal shouts. "Every night, they keep coming up the canyon!" Cal wipes roughly at his face. "And you won't let me do anything about it."

Mom's mouth opens and shuts but nothing comes out. Then she looks down at the gun in her hands. She storms upstairs where we hear the slamming and locking of closet doors.

Cal slams out the back door.

Gramps, muttering, starts shuffling back to the kitchen. He waves his hand around as if he's had it with the whole business.

And I'm still standing right where I came in, clutching my backpack full of comics in my cramped fingers, my mouth hanging open.

What the heck am I supposed to do now?

Mom solves the problem. "Stanley!" she shouts from upstairs. "GO FEED THE CHICKENS!"

The coop's past the garden beds, alongside the detached garage—a green, slanty-roofed wooden hut with eight hens. Gramps built it for us after he got here last year, and Dad, when he came over to help, teased him. "Why don't you just mail all the neighborhood coyotes an engraved dinner party invitation," he'd joked.

But somehow, miraculously, we haven't lost a chicken yet.

I head out there with a bowl of kitchen veggie scraps, and whistle for Albert Einstein, who is snuffling in the underbrush. "Stay away from there, Albert Einstein! That's coyote territory!"

He totally ignores me.

"ALBERT EINSTEIN!" He is too busy circling and

snuffling. Finally, he chooses a primo piece of real estate and squats. When he's done, he won't come back to me, so I have to drag him by the collar.

He's lucky he's at least good looking.

I put down the scrap bowl and I'm just turning to pry open the chicken feed bin when I hear a small cough—and what do you know, there she is again, the Axi-Tun warrior girl, standing by the corner of our garage.

Liberty.

Great.

"So, why you are yelling at the top of your lungs for Albert Einstein?" she asks. "Urgent physics questions?"

I point to the dog, who stares at me with his glazed, button-like eyes. "That's his name. It's ironic." I grab a scoop of pellets, pick up the scrap bowl, then open the latch of the run with my elbow. The flock squawks and gathers around my ankles, ruffling their feathers.

"Wow," she says. "I've never seen chickens this close up—except on my plate."

"They really like their pecking order," I tell her. "See that big one? That's Henrietta. She's the bossy, popular girl. She makes sure she gets fed first."

"Huh," Liberty says. "There's one of those in every school, too, isn't there?" She snorts. "So, say, which one would be the school bully?"

I laugh. "Probably Omeletta. Watch out. She'll go

after you." We probably should have named her Kyle Keefner.

"What about those two?" Liberty points to the newest flock members, two poor puny hens we've nicknamed Chick and Fil-A. Chick is missing some feathers—Gramps says she plucks them out herself, from stress. Birds can do that.

"Well," I say, "they're at the end of the line. I guess they're a bit like me and my friend, Joon, to be honest. Although Joon is moving up in the pecking order."

Liberty takes the scrap bowl from me, wrinkling her nose at the tangy smell coming off the potato peels and rotten apple rinds. "So he's moving up, but you're not?" She nudges the two straggler chickens with her foot. "Seriously. Why even keep track? Pecking orders are for chickens."

Try telling that to Joon, I think to myself. But I don't say anything.

On Monday morning, we've barely set foot in the building before Principal Coffin calls an all-school pep rally and sports safety presentation.

Ugh.

I head straight to the main office, down the little hall to my Ready Room.

It's been a week since I've left it. The sketchpad is still

there, and I don't waste time breaking out the markers. I shut the door against the buzz and noise of kids in the hall, heading down to assembly.

Might as well kill time drawing.

Joon and the Trivia Quest are heavy on my mind. This is something that should be fun, right? I know a ton of trivia! But I have this feeling, like Joon is throwing it down as an unspoken dare. Do this with him, or else. Prove myself. Or else.

Every time I think of doing the Quest with Joon, worries sprout in me like tree branches. I'm like Groot, the tree creature from Guardians of the Galaxy. I can sprout worry-branches so fast, it's—worrisome.

9

THINGS HAVE BEEN pretty quiet this week. Cal's been too busy with football and soccer to spend much time torturing me. Mom's been working constantly. We haven't heard from Dad in a while. And I don't see Liberty around at all. At home, it's mainly just Gramps and me, hanging out in different parts of the house.

The sort of good thing is that Joon asked me over on Saturday again, to prepare for the Trivia Quest.

The sort of bad thing is that now that I'm here, he's totally distracted.

"Come on!" I say. "You should know this one. Who's Martian Manhunter's archenemy?"

"Wait. Who's Martian Manhunter again?" Joon says, fiddling with his phone.

"Just mute it. Why does it keep buzzing?"

But Joon ignores me and keeps texting.

I go sit at his desk. I take my own phone out of my pocket, and look at the blank screen.

Why do I even have this thing? No one ever calls me. Not even my mom.

There's a big stack of paper on Joon's desk—I take a sheet, just to kill time while he texts. I'm doodling, just putting down lines, and suddenly, a superhero starts to emerge. I give him a grey spandex suit, a big blue utility belt, and a flowing bright-blue cape.

BY STANLEY

I only look up when Joon hits me in the head with a dirty sock. "What are you drawing?" He comes to look. I try to hide it but I'm too slow.

"Dude!" Joon says, prying the paper from my hands and laughing. "Good thing the Trivia Quest isn't an art contest.'"

"It was just an idea I had," I mutter, jumping for it. But Joon holds it high out of reach, playing keep-away. Since when did Joon get so much taller than me?

"Give it back!" I yell.

He takes a closer look. "You know what?" Joon says, tilting his head and holding the paper at arm's length. "This is not too shabby, Fart-in-bra. You've got the arms and legs the right proportion, anyway."

"Who are you, Kyle Keefner? Stop it!" I jump for the paper again, and miss.

He ignores me and turns, frowning at the sketch. "Who's it supposed to be? What superhero?"

"Not your business," I say, a little too loudly. I'm getting steamed.

"The face," he says, peering. "You know what? It sorta looks like your dad."

I stop jumping. I put out my hand and command him: "Gimme that back."

Something in my voice must finally make him listen. Because he does.

10

THE FOLLOWING MONDAY, Mrs. Green makes me read my Greek Myth essay aloud. (I wrote about how Prometheus stole fire from the gods, who punished him by having a bird peck out his liver. I said it was about how mankind's always yearned for superpowers, and she raved about it until all the other kids wanted to peck out MY liver.)

Then, Wednesday, in Accelerated Math, they move me to a new eighth-grade class for a unit on graphs and slopes. Guess where I had to sit? Right in front of Cal. I thought he was going to peck out my liver, too.

On Thursday, Liberty Silverberg skateboards on her driveway until dark, trying kick-flips and wiping out until her uncle opens a window and yells, "Do I have to call your mother?" The sound of her wheels was super-distracting and loud. I could barely do my home-work.

Now it's Friday morning. If I can just get through today . . .

"Surprise!" Principal Coffin says over the PA speaker.

Mrs. Green tilts her head back and looks like she's pleading with the ceiling.

"We'll be having an armed intruder drill in five min-utes, folks! It is just a drill! Your teachers are prepared! There is no need to be worried . . ."

A flashing dazzle of light catches my eye outside the classroom windows. It's reflecting off the metal bumper of a police car just turning into the drive.

"Listen to your teachers and follow their instructions very carefully. Afterward, I'd like everyone to head to the auditorium for a breakdown of how it went."

A restless murmur buzzes around the room. And a tiny Red Alert pings through my system: woop. Woop.

Intruder? I imagine guns.

Kids huddled together, scared.

Bullets fired down a hall—

RAT–TAT–TAT! BANG! ZOOM! POW! . . .

Mrs. Green nods at me. As I shove my notebook into my backpack, I hear Kyle Keefner mutter, "Stay con-scious, Fart-in-bra!" Mrs. Green shushes him, but kids are already laughing.

Principal Coffin continues on the PA as I walk down the hall. "Your teacher will direct you to the designated safe corner of your classroom. You will shelter in place until the all clear is sounded."

I push open the main office door and see two police officers standing at the counter. In their black uniforms, gun belts, and gear, they look like two of Gotham City's finest. Batman and Commissioner Gordon could show up any minute now.

"I am going to say a code phrase," Principal Coffin continues over the intercom. "Remember, this is a drill; this is only a drill. But if you ever hear me say this code phrase again, it means we are having a real crisis, and you need to do exactly what your teachers tell you."

Woop. I try not to let my stupid branching fear-thoughts in. Intrusive thoughts of intruders.

"Never repeat this phrase to strangers," Principal Coffin warns. "If there's ever serious trouble afoot at Peavey, these are the secret code words you will hear . . ."

There's a long pause, like she's hearing an imaginary drumroll or something. Then Principal Coffin announces, in a bold, crisp voice:

"John Lockdown! Please report for duty!"

John Lockdown. That's funny. I imagine a James

Bond type in a tuxedo, drinking a martini and saying: "The name's Lockdown. John Lockdown." Or ducking down the sixth-grade hallway, brandishing a revolver. A suave, school catastrophe-averting superhero dude.

Wow.

The intercom clicks off. There's the faint sound of hundreds of chairs scraping back as kids all over the school get up from their seats. Then the alarm system starts beeping, like the whole building is having a panic attack. I watch as Gotham's finest police officers stride quickly out into the hall with Principal Coffin.

There's a hand on my shoulder. I jump.

It's Mrs. Ngozo. She hands me a brochure called *Intruder Alert! School Under Attack! Here's What to Do!* as well as a package of soft, squishy earplugs. "Look," she says. "I've got them in, too." She pulls back her braids to show me.

I stuff them in my ears and head to my Ready Room. It's just as I left it: desk, chair, easel, sketchpad. I shove the brochure into a desk drawer. Then I flip open the pad.

Wait.

62

There's nothing, no name. It's a mystery artist. Who did this?

And what do they mean about their super-senses turning into superpowers?

Look at that superhero they drew. A grey suit. A blue utility belt. His bright-blue cape . . . It's almost the same outfit I drew on my superhero doodle, back at Joon's house the other day.

What are the odds of that?

The skin on my neck and the backs of my arms start to prickle. Maybe there really is a real, live, school catastrophe-averting superhero out there! Someone who can keep bad guys out! Make sure kids don't get bullied or hurt. That they're not forced into sensory overload. A real superhero. A real . . . John Lockdown.

Yeah.

A superhero who stands up for the little guy. For kids who are human targets in dodgeball. The ones not invited to parties. The gossiped about. The lonely lunch-eaters.

John Lockdown.

A shiver runs down my back.

I turn the page, pick up a marker, and start drawing like crazy. Before you know it, I've got a few rough frames. It's basically stick figures, but it's the start of a story—my first real comic.

I call it:

From super-senses to superpowers, a superhero for our times . . .

Never fear—

JOHN LOCKDOWN
IS IN THE BUILDING!

(Who is John Lockdown?)

BY STANLEY

The third period bell rings before I know it.

On my way out Mrs. Ngozo looks up from her desk. "Everything good?"

"Oh, yeah. Yes, ma'am." I quickly take out my earplugs.

"Did you do your breathing?" she says. "Aqua, ochre?"

I nod. Then I pause by her door. I really want to know who this mystery artist could be but I don't want to reveal anything, either. The sketchpad, I want it to be my own secret.

"Mrs. Ngozo," I ask, "who else uses this room? I mean—does anyone else spend time in here?"

"Ahhhhh," she says, closing her laptop and looking at me meaningfully. "I see what you mean."

My heart quickens.

"I'm sorry. The answer is no, Stanley." She smiles. "No one else uses that room. You're the only one. But there's absolutely nothing wrong with needing a safe, quiet zone at school. You have a legitimate disorder! A sensory disorder! So do not worry. Believe me, young man, you have absolutely nothing whatsoever to be ashamed of."

"Oh yeah," I say quickly. "Okay. Thanks."

Yeah, shame. I'd almost forgotten about shame.

11

FART–IN–BRA! KYLE SHOUTS the minute I perch my butt at the edge of the bench in the lunchroom. Why didn't Joon save me a seat? He's all the way at the other end of the table, next to Dylan Bustamante. I try to catch his eye, but he's too fascinated by his sandwich.

"You missed it!" Kyle goes on. "One of the cops showed us his gun. He said he was actually at a school shooting. It was awesome."

The other guys just grunt, busy slurping their milk and cramming pizza in their mouths. Joon still doesn't look up. I try to act cool, like I don't mind being called Fart-in-bra and talking about school shootings.

"We're all supposed to run away from the building

if we can," Dylan says. "Or if not, then the second thing we're supposed to do is hide. Or if not, and it's life or death, then we're supposed to gang up and attack the shooter. Last-ditch effort. Maybe take him down."

"Ha!" says Keefner. "Can you imagine Fart-in-bra ganging up on an armed suspect?" Keefner screws his face up like a baby crying, and mimics me beating up a bad guy, like I'm shaking tiny maracas. Everyone laughs.

Even Joon.

It takes forever for the seventh period bell to ring. I go to the bus, thinking about how Joon's going to flip when I tell him about the mystery artist. About John Lockdown, and the Sketchpad of Mystery.

But as I head down the bus aisle, I can't believe it! Dylan Bustamante is in my seat.

I don't want to be jealous but, come on, the guy raps his pencil on the edge of his desk in Language Arts, rat-a-tat-tat, rat-a-tat-tat, over and over, and it drives everyone crazy. Also, he laughs at everything Kyle Keefner says. He wears muscle shirts for gym because he's deluded and thinks that he has good biceps. And he reeks of Cleaver body spray.

Joon's laughing at something Dylan said. I catch his eye. He gives me a thumbs-up and the quickest flash of a guilty look. "Catch you later, Stan . . . It's cool, right?"

Cool? That Dylan Blubber-Head Bust-a-Face Busta-mante is sitting in my seat?

The kid behind me knees me, and I stumble on. "Sure, no big," I call back to him. "Hey—I have something interesting to tell you tomorrow."

"What's tomorrow?"

I stare at him, unbelieving. "Saturday? Hanging out? Trivia Quest?"

"Oh yeah," Joon says, frowning, and scratching at his gel-spiked hair. "Great!"

I keep walking to the back of the bus.

Something's up. The way Joon just said "great"?

It wasn't so great.

When Cal and I get home, Mom's out by the garage, in her work clothes, talking to the neighbor girl, Liberty. I haven't seen her in almost a week. She's got a baseball cap on, and a T-shirt that says, *If you see someone crying, ask them if it's because of their haircut.*

Mom's got Dad's toolbox out, and the tall ladder leaning against the garage. A big cardboard box is open on the grass. "Calvin, Stanley, come look!" she calls. "I ordered motion-sensor lights! Maybe they'll keep the coyotes out of the yard at night!"

As we walk over, Liberty says, "Hope it works. The

noises at night around here freak me out. Those weird, creepy yips."

"Yeah, they do that to surround their prey," says Cal. "They disorient it before closing in and tearing it to shreds. We're talking rabbits, opossum, sometimes cats and small dogs." He's using his bossy, know-it-all voice. Liberty pretends to listen politely. Then, when Cal's not looking, she turns to me and crosses her eyes.

I try not to smile.

She steadies one side of the ladder, and I hold the other.

"This isn't going to work, Mom," Cal says. "The only thing they'll respect is a rifle."

Liberty frowns. "Respect?"

Mom looks down sternly from the top step and points Dad's electric drill in the general direction of Cal's forehead. "If you're not going to help with the lights, Calvin, go inside and start your homework. Stanley, hold this ladder steady!"

"Coyotes don't attack people, do they?" Liberty asks.

"There's absolutely nothing to worry about," Mom says firmly.

"Then why are you installing motion sensors?" I say.

Mom just sighs and starts up the drill.

12

WEEK BY WEEK, day by day, the Trivia Quest approacheth. It's Saturday morning, so I'm making toast and getting ready to call Joon so we can study. Calvin is slurping down cereal and milk. Gramps is clutching his coffee mug and muttering about the stock market, and Mom's scrolling through her phone screen.

"Hey—here's something from your father," she says. "Listen to this. He's in Nairobi, meeting with microfinance people. He says 'This is turning into a multi-village project and a new cooperative venture for both the financial side and the villagers involved' . . ." Her voice trails off.

Gramps harrumphs from his spot at the table. "You'd think that man would ask about the home front every

71

once in a while," he says, moving his jaw like he's chewing on each word before spitting it out.

I don't want to think about Dad. It just makes my stomach hurt. I grab my toast and go in the other room to call Joon.

"Stanley." Joon's voice sounds surprised. "Hey, funny you should call."

"What's so funny about it?" I say. "Saturday's our playdate day." A flash of annoyance hits me.

"Dude, seriously. Don't ever say the word 'playdate.'"

My face flushes hot. "Right—sorry."

"Thing is," Joon goes on, "Dylan slept over . . . and we have soccer later." He covers the phone; there's muffled talking.

"Well, okay. Come over for a little while, anyway. And bring your Silver Surfers? And some Captain Marvels? That'd be cool."

It's so hot, by the time I get there I'm drenched. Joon slides open his window and says, "Dude! We're coming down. Meet us out back."

I sit on the edge of a lounge chair under a tree and grab a Silver Surfer at random from my pack. It's the one about the Ultimate Nullifier—an artifact the Human Torch brought back from Galactus's world-ship, Taa II. The Ultimate Nullifier doesn't just destroy, it un-exists things. Which is a very cool idea for a weapon.

What kind of superweapons should John Lockdown carry? Maybe the bottles of cleaning chemicals on the shelves in the utility closet are supernatural solutions that make the stuff he cleans turn invisible. Or bullet-proof. Or impervious to pain and suffering.

When I get back to the Sketchpad of Mystery, I'll work on that.

Ten minutes go by before the back door clicks open. Joon has his old red nylon sports bag slung over his shoulder, and Dylan's standing right behind him.

"Stan!" Joon says, looking down at me. "Really sorry, dude—it's actually way later than I thought it was. Dylan and I have soccer, and we have to go over to his place to pick up his stuff." Joon shifts the bag around, keeping his eyes on the ground. "Sorry about the change of plans."

I wait for him to say, "You want to come with?" or "How about tomorrow?" But he doesn't say anything. He—they—just stand there, staring at me, like they're hoping I'll Disapparate like Harry Potter or something.

My heart starts pounding. It's not a Red Alert of fear. It's Red Anger. "What about preparing for the Trivia Quest?"

Joon looks quickly away. "I still care about the

Quest," he says.

"Wait—are you talking about that Trivia Quest they keep advertising? The Comic Fest thing? You guys are doing that?" Dylan asks.

Joon nods.

"That's cool!" Dylan says. "I'd totally do that."

"Really? You would?" says Joon. His eyebrows shoot up into his new, spiky hairline, and he breaks into a big smile. Bigger than any smile I've seen on his face lately.

Then Joon turns back to me. "Stanley, really sorry about today. You want to just lend me those comics, and we'll pick it up later?" He reaches out his hands for the stack I'm holding.

But I don't hand them over. Instead I clutch them to my chest and turn away. (True, they're mainly just Silver Surfers from the 2014 series and some relatively unimportant Captain Marvels, but there are a couple of really good ones in there, and I don't feel like sharing anymore.)

I turn and go. I walk really fast down his drive and break into a run on the sidewalk. I blow past the mail guy and leave Mrs. Martinez, the fastest power-walker in the neighborhood, in my dust.

All I want is to be back in my safe, calm room. Immediately.

As I fly by, I see Liberty Silverberg sitting in a big

chair on her porch, reading. She stands up and smiles at me. She raises her hand and shouts, "Hail, Norm!"

The whole Norm thing? Not funny.

I ignore her. I slam the back door behind me and fly up the stairs and down the hall to my room, my safe space. I shut the window blinds, fling down onto the bed, and cover my head with a pillow.

I need darkness. Silence. My head is banging and pulsing with heat and anger. I need silence in order to process what just happened:

I just got un-existed by my best friend.

13

I DON'T EMERGE from my room until almost dinnertime, when I can't ignore the fact that unusual smells are wafting under my door. Ah yes. If my distant memories of days gone by are correct, that is the distinct aroma of . . . home cooking!

"There you are," Mom says, darting me a quick glance as I come in the kitchen. "You feeling okay?"

"I'm fine, Mom."

"Then wash these greens. I've asked our new neighbors to dinner. Chicken parm, and a cake's in the oven."

Chicken parm! Cake! My heart lifts! Then it sinks again, at the thought of Liberty. "Did you have to?" I say. "Can't we just eat it all ourselves?"

Mom ignores me and digs in the back of the cupboard

for spices. "Should we ask the Lees, too? I've got plenty of food. Liberty could meet Joon."

Woop! A panic blip. "No!" I shout. "I mean, I think they're already busy."

"If you say so." Mom wipes her hands on her apron and frowns at me. "Everything okay with Joon?"

"What? Yeah," I lie. "Of course! Totally fine."

Mothers are psychic.

At exactly six, Gramps, Cal, and I are all in clean shirts, looking miserable, and Mom's whipping off her apron as the doorbell rings.

Liberty and her uncle are almost as tall as the doorway. She's clutching a box of chocolates in her bony hands. Her T-shirt says, *Sorry I'm late. I didn't want to come.*

Dr. Silverberg is huge, with stooped shoulders, balding red hair, and a big grin. He hands Mom a bottle of wine and starts chatting away before he's even in the door. Not only is he big, but he also has very big expressions—his eyes widen and his brows shoot up a lot when he talks. His face is like an exclamation point.

"Thanks so much for having us!" he says. "So glad to be part of the neighborhood!" Liberty mimicks him behind his back as he goes on and on. I try not to smile.

Over dinner, Dr. Silverberg tells us he's a new doctor at the hospital—it's his first job out of med school.

He tells us all about his work! And about how he found an Excellent! Homeschool! Tutor! For Liberty! Through the university! She rolls her eyes at the word 'excellent,' and chomps down harder on her piece of garlic bread.

Then Gramps starts talking about the weather. How bad it is in the Midwest compared to Pennsylvania, where the Silverbergs lived before here. "I can sure feel the weather and dampness in this bum shoulder of mine," he grumbles, and actually gets Dr. Silverberg to get up out of his chair and examine it, right there in the middle of dinner, while Mom tries to politely protest.

After Gramps's shoulder is looked at, Dr. Silverberg sits back down and takes second helpings. He mentions wanting to learn how to surf, and Calvin tells him about a few good spots.

Meanwhile, every time I catch her eye, Liberty imitates her uncle. It's not mean—you can tell she likes him. But I'm trying hard not to laugh.

"Liberty, honey, would you like more?" Mom says.

"Yes, please, ma'am." She passes over her empty plate. "Everything's delicious."

"My mom's an excellent cook when she cooks, which is never," says Cal in a way deeper voice than usual.

"It's so nice to see Liberty with a good appetite again," says Dr. Silverberg, sitting back and patting his own belly.

"Again?" says Mom, smiling politely, eyebrows raised.

There's an awkward pause. Liberty stops with her fork halfway to her mouth. Dr. Silverberg looks at her, and then at Mom, and his face flushes red. Neither of them say anything more. And Mom quickly changes the subject.

But after that, Liberty stops smirking and mimicking and trying to make me laugh. She just stares straight ahead and waits for the visit to end.

14

MONDAY MORNING, I don't even try to sit with Joon on the bus. Dylan's in my usual spot. I sit farther back so I can bore Superman-eyeball heat-vision laser holes into the backs of their two stupid heads.

I spend the ride to school thinking about what galactic weapon I'd use to eradicate Bustamante's existence. If I had Mjolnir, Thor's hammer, I'd summon a storm, or send him hurtling into some hideous new dimension where the evil forces of the universe would punish him for not knowing superhero trivia. If I had Wolverine's adamantium claws, well, I'm probably a little too squeamish for the Wolverine approach.

Hellboy's Samaritan gun? Daredevil's billy club? Or maybe something from Batman's utility belt—there's a crazy treasure trove of stuff in there. Batarangs, a grapple gun, a cryptographic sequencer, tracers, smoke and gas pellets, a tranquilizer gun, glue, line launchers, lock picks, a laser, various grenades, SONIC DEVASTATORS . . . even Kryptonite.

I bet Joon and Dylan couldn't name one-quarter of what's in Batman's belt.

I cruise up the walk past Joon and Dylan, who pretend not to notice me, and stomp down the hall into Mrs. Green's homeroom.

"Gooood morning, Peavey Schoooul!" booms Principal Coffin over the scratchy PA.

Now I feel like smacking my head on my desk.

"Surprise! You never know when it's time for a safety drill! Remember, we must always be prepared for the worst! Expect the best, prepare for the worst, that's our Peavey motto," she says .

Red Alert!

Red Alert!

I can't wait to go to the office, escape the madness, and visit the Sketchpad of Mystery. But I've only just raised my hand when the classroom door bursts open.

Everyone gasps.

My brother, Calvin, of all people, is standing there. And he has smears of blood on his face.

"Oh my God!" Some of the girls let out a quick, surprised shriek. Because in his two outstretched arms he's carrying an unconscious kid.

My heart starts pounding like a bird got trapped in my chest and is trying to flap its frantic way out. I grip the sides of my desk so hard the joints in my fingers ache.

Calvin has a strange expression on his face—grim, but his mouth's twitching like he's trying to keep from smiling. He rushes forward into our classroom and clunks the injured kid down on the front table. The boy's head lolls off the edge. Cal yanks him back by the ankles.

It's a CPR dummy, of course. Ugh. Seriously, did they have to use fake blood? Principal Coffin is going to end up giving me an actual heart attack. That's going to be the only real emergency at Peavey: me, having a heart attack from an overdose of emergency preparedness.

The CPR dummy boy lies sprawled out on the table. Cal jerks his thumb at it, then at us. "WHO IN THIS CLASS COULD STEP UP RIGHT NOW AND DO PROPER CPR ON THIS KID, IF THIS WAS A REAL EMERGENCY?" he says in his big-shot, eighth-grade, know-it-all voice.

There are sounds out in the hall of other classrooms getting their CPR dummy visits. Clunk, clunk, go dolls on tables. I know this is just a super-dramatic way to make a point, but still—STILL! I'm starting to feel sea-sick. I imagine putting my mouth on that gross rubbery doll mouth. The fake, clotted blood that looks like lumpy dark ketchup.

Uh-oh.

I think I'm gonna barf.

I lurch up from my desk. My gag reflex is kicking in. My stomach is telling me I have about five seconds to get to the boys' room. I stumble blindly past desks, sprint down the hall. I almost make it.

But not quite.

"Oh, Stanley, you poor thing," Mrs. Green says, coming out of our classroom and over to where I'm crouched, miserable, near the water fountain. "I'll call for cleanup. Do you think you can get yourself to the office?"

By the time I've straightened up and pulled myself together, the custodian is already on his way, wheeling along one of those mop-and-pail carts. Same guy from when I fainted in the fire drill. It figures.

"Sorry about that," I mumble at my shoes, which thank goodness missed getting barfed on.

"You better be sorry, dork." It's Calvin's voice ringing out from behind me. "Your teacher just told me to walk you to the office. Thanks for ruining my talk."

I don't say anything, I just keep walking while Calvin

tears into me. "Do you have to be such a weenie? Why are you the only kid who can't hack it?"

I stop in the middle of the hall. It's hard to breathe, but not just from panic. Also from shock at Calvin's anger.

"You barely talk! And everything upsets you," Cal shouts. He gives me a small shove so I stumble back against the cinder-block wall. "You're an embarrassment, Stannie. And don't hold your hands up by your chest like two little paws." He squints at me, disgusted. "You've been doing that your whole life, and it's so stupid! You're almost thirteen. You're in *my* school now. Grow up!"

I yank my hands down to my sides and growl, "Leave me alone, Cal."

"Gladly," he says. And with a loud pivoting squeak of his sneaker, he takes off back down the hall.

The school secretaries glance at me over their reading glasses as I slip past, to the Ready Room.

Cal's words still burn and roil around inside me. I'm pretty used to him being a jerk. But this was the worst ever.

The Sketchpad of Mystery sits in the corner, closed. I can't bear to open it until my churning stomach and angry head settle.

But when I finally do go uncover the pad, this is what I see.

15

JOON CALLS RIGHT before dinner that night.

"Stan?" he says. "I'm sorry about Saturday."

My shoulders relax for the first time in days. I take a deep breath. "Whoa. Me too! I'm so glad you called. It's just—"

"Yeah. It's just, you know, I've been thinking. Really thinking. About the Quest."

I hold my breath.

"Maybe it's better if just Dylan and I enter it."

I freeze.

"—I mean, you're great at the trivia, Stan," he goes on. "We all know that. Really amazing at trivia, and thanks for helping me with all those charts and stuff." Joon's words are coming out in a rush. "But let's face it.

You'd never survive the day downtown. It's too much for you, right?"

My heart hammers. My voice cracks. "But—it's Trivia Quest! You need me to win!"

"Yeah, well," Joon says softly. "I also just want to have fun!"

My whole world stops. Goes silent. "I'm fun!" I say, but it comes out as a croak. "Name one time I wasn't fun."

"One time?" Joon actually laughs. "Just one? How about, for starters, the school dance last month?"

"What did I do?" I whisper.

"You complained the music was too loud—"

"It was!"

"—So we went outside to get away from it, and then Kyle and Dylan followed us, and we wanted to have a rolling race down the back hill in those empty garbage pails. Remember?"

"Filthy garbage cans, dude. That was dangerous."

"You told on us!"

"Well, the chaperones asked where you went! What was I gonna do, lie? And I was worried. You could have gotten hurt!"

"See? That's what I mean. Why couldn't you just roll with us?"

I sputter. But I was saving him from danger!

"—And then there was last year, when I explained to you who likes who. And you turned it into a flow chart."

I groan.

"—With arrows and boxes, and, like, ten different colors, to explain what girl liked what boy. And everybody saw it, and some girls cried. You made girls cry, dude!"

My insides are curdling with humiliation. My face is on fire. "Okay, I agree. That was really stupid, I know."

"Stanley. Come on. We're at Peavey now. You have to learn how to handle stuff."

First Calvin. Now Joon? I clench my hands, jump up, and suddenly I'm shouting back at him. "I can handle stuff! You have no idea!" My heart is pounding. "And you know what? You stink at being a friend! And you know what else? I can do the Trivia Quest all by myself, Joon! And win it, too! I don't need you! In fact, you'd hold me back! I'm going to enter it and beat you! So there!"

"FINE!"

"FINE!" I slam down the phone and listen to the blood pound, pound, pound in my ears.

When the waves of outrage finally stop crashing, a super-heavy sadness drifts in and settles over me.

I wish John Lockdown were real. If he were here, right now, maybe he could weave some kind of magic power over me and Joon, and make things go back to how they used to be, when we were younger. Before Peavey.

But John Lockdown doesn't exist. And we're not younger. We're older. And I'm all out of ideas how to fix this mess.

I guess from now on, as to Joon and me? We're done.

And another thing:

I think I'm stuck entering the Trivia Quest.

16

MOM'S LATE for dinner again. Really late. We've been keeping the delivery pizza boxes warm in the oven for such a long time, the kitchen smells like hot cardboard, not pizza. I pull the boxes out before she even takes off her red blazer.

"Boys. There's new coyote scat all over our driveway," Mom says, dropping her briefcase and giving Albert Einstein a pat. "When you see that out there, you should clean it up."

"Darn straight they should, the lazy apes," says Gramps, hunched over in his chair, already munching on a slice. "I told 'em. I told these boys, get to work." Actually he hasn't told us anything. He's been in his recliner watching *The History of Hydraulics* all afternoon.

"Yo, coyote scat is disgusting. It's, like, full of nuts and rocks and stuff," Calvin says with a disgusting half-chewed wad of pepperoni hanging half out of his mouth.

"The motion-sensor lights aren't scaring them off?" I ask.

Mom shakes her head.

Cal says, in his deep, know-it-all voice, "You know, I could solve the whole problem. Just a few warning shots over their heads! I'm talking warning shots!"

"That might do it," Gramps says, nodding.

Mom bangs her hand down hard on the table, and all conversation stops.

After dinner I hang out in my room and try not to think about Joon. Every time I do, a little whirlwind of anger and sadness spins around in my chest. The feelings are so mixed up, I don't know the mad from the sad. All I know is that I've got to prove that I'm cool. And capable. And don't need anyone. That I can handle the Trivia Quest, and beat Joon. I want to win those passes, so I can throw them in Joon's face.

I've printed the entry form. I just need Mom to sign it.

I think about John Lockdown. About what he said. About finding your superpowers when you least expect it. He found his in a utility room. I need to find mine—somehow. Somewhere. I need to believe it's possible to change.

So when Mom heads up into her room, I figure it's now or never. I'm going to do it. I'm going to ask her to sign my form.

I take some deep breaths—aqua, ochre, aqua, ochre—and I'm about to knock on her door, when I overhear her angry voice.

"That's unbelievable. How could you make that commitment?" Her voice is low, but loud enough so that I can hear it through the door. I stand there, frozen. "What do I tell the boys?" she says. "YOU tell the boys."

She's talking to Dad on the phone.

Now her voice is muffled—she's probably moved toward her bathroom. I strain to listen but I can't make anything else out.

I back away slowly and tiptoe down the hall, down the stairs, and through the kitchen, still clutching my Trivia Quest application form. I head outside to breathe some fresh air.

What did Mom mean? What the heck does Dad have to tell us?

I realize what I'm doing. My feet are trying to head over to Joon's house, to tell him about it. I catch myself just before I turn down the sidewalk—and then I feel even worse about everything.

I pace up and down our driveway instead. The air is cooling off by the minute, now the sun's down, and a dry wind starts me sneezing. I bend over, prepping for the usual marathon—my record's sixty-seven sneezes, back in fourth grade. Joon counted them for me.

"Hey." A voice comes from Liberty's kitchen window. "Pretty impressive snot expulsion."

She comes down her back steps and stands there staring with her bulgy eyes. Her T-shirt says, *The Sports Team from My Geographical Region Is Superior to the Sports Team from Your Geographical Region.* She frowns at me, then digs in her pocket to offer me a suspiciously rumpled Kleenex.

"Nah. I'm fine. My mom just said something weird, that's all. I'm over it."

Her face softens a little. "Moms. Gotta love 'em."

I straighten up and wipe my nose on the back of my hand. "So . . . why do you live with your uncle?"

Her eyebrows shoot up. "Well, I usually live with my mom. But Uncle Dan's always been kind of my second parent." She digs the toe of her flip-flop into the grass. "Sometimes Mom's needed a break from me—back when she used to be this free-spirit hippie mom. So I'd go live with Uncle Dan for a while." She looks up at the pine tree, frowning. "But Mom's way more uptight now. These days it's *me* who needs the break from *her*."

"Yeah? Why did it change?"

Liberty shrugs. She places her hand on the tree trunk. "Let's just say, my mom's gone from free-spirit to total control freak, where I'm concerned." She picks off a piece of pine bark. "So I asked to come here. I had to get out of her clutches."

"Well, that's good, I guess," I say. "Your uncle seems, uh, cool."

I watch her flick pieces of bark off the tree. Finally, she shrugs. "He's fine." Then she sighs, turns, and points to my shirt. "What's that?"

I perk up at the change of subject. "It's an old vintage comic detective dude named Dick Tracy," I tell her. "This picture? It was drawn in 1941. See his old-fashioned hat and trench coat? But now, look at his wristwatch. It's not far off from today's smartwatch, right? This was totally impossible sci-fi in the 1940s. Like wildest dreams. Like fiction. Now it's the norm."

"You don't say, Norm." She chucks me on the shoulder. "I wonder what kind of stuff will be the norm in the future."

"Yeah," I nod. "Comics are a kick. They've predicted

all kinds of stuff." The image of John Lockdown suddenly flashes through my head.

"So," she says, pointing at my shirt again. "I take it you're into them. Comics, I mean."

And just like that, I start telling her. About how great comics are. How Joon and I always were into them together—it was our thing. But we fought over Trivia Quest, and now we're not friends.

I tell her about how much I hate Peavey—except for the Ready Room, the Sketchpad of Mystery, and the ongoing adventures of John Lockdown. How I keep thinking about him, all the story lines he could have. I have a ton of ideas to share with the mystery artist. Stories about all the ways John Lockdown could save us.

How I have this weird feeling he's here, in some strange way, to help save *me*.

Liberty's quiet as I talk. Finally, she smiles at me, pats my shoulder and says, "Who knows? Maybe your John Lockdown is real. My mom, you know, she believes in spirits and stuff. She says we have to watch what we think because our spirits can turn our wishes into real things, and put them out into the world. Maybe your superhero's out there somewhere already."

"That would be weird but cool," I say.

"Yup. Weird but cool," she says, looking off into

the distance. "Just like my mom,"
And just like her, I think.
But I don't say it.

17

THE NEXT AFTERNOON I'm at the kitchen table doing homework when Albert Einstein starts barking at his dog dish.

Apparently it's because Liberty's at the kitchen door, holding a paper shopping bag.

I let her in, and she stands there by the counter, shifting from one giant foot to another, clumsily patting Albert Einstein's head.

"Here," she says, handing me the bag. "This was in one of Uncle Dan's moving boxes. He said it's okay to lend them to you. I read a few. Pretty entertainingly . . . old."

I open the bag and it's filled with old comics. Archie and Jughead from the 1970s. A Spider-Man from 1991, and one mega-super-old intriguing-looking comic called the Clock, with a guy in a wide-shouldered suit and a black mask, holding a flashlight. They reek of basement mildew, but: wow!

"They're probably not valuable or anything," she says, "but I was thinking about that Trivia Quest thing you talked about. Maybe they'll help."

I'm grinning so hard my cheeks hurt. "I'll be careful with them." I thumb through the pages. "I've definitely heard of some of these but I've never actually seen them before. Way cool."

I look up to thank her, but she's already slipped back out the door.

Next morning, when I head down for breakfast, a weird sight greets me: Mom. Still at home. Sitting at the table drinking coffee with Gramps.

"Did you get fired or something?" I say, wondering if this is the right time to ask her to sign my Trivia Quest form.

"I'm going in late. And I'll drive you boys to school today," she says, glancing at her wristwatch as Cal stomps down the steps behind me.

Gramps is shaking his head disapprovingly.

"I want you and your brother to sit down and have a little chat with your dad this morning," Mom says. "He has some news for you."

Cal, his nose already in the fridge, calls out, "I emailed Dad about the rifle. Bet he's gonna say to let me have it."

"I'll let you have it," mutters Gramps.

Mom holds up her hand. "I want you to give your dad some respect for what he has to say." She angles the laptop so that both Cal and I can see the screen.

I think about what I overheard in Mom's room. I don't have a good feeling about this.

"Hey, guys!" Dad's crackly voice emerges from the speaker, and his face peers out at us. He's really tan, and he's wearing a hat, so it's hard to make out his expression. Also, he's shaved off his goatee. He barely looks like Dad.

"Wow, Dad. It's been so . . . long," I say.

He nods, tilts his head, clears his throat, smiles a little. "It has, and I'm really sorry about that. You know how much I miss you, don't you? But you know how important this work is. It's life or death, quite frankly."

Something Principal Coffin would say.

"Anyhow" —Dad stops to clear his throat—"I wanted to tell you that it's looking like I need to stay on a bit longer than planned. Quite a bit longer."

Something drops in the pit of my stomach.

"What? Nooo!" Cal roars. He's suddenly bright red. "But you've been gone for months!"

Gramps shakes his head and mutters to the newspaper.

Dad takes off his hat and scratches at his head. Whoa—his hair's so long, he's got a ponytail now. A ponytail.

I let out my breath. And suddenly, I'm as mad as Cal. So mad, I feel like throwing my chair across the room.

Who is this person, and what did he do with my dad?

"It's been a very, very tough decision to have to make, boys," he says. "But the foundation pulled funding at the last minute from two big projects, and we're scrambling. I need to stay on. I need to keep my word to these people. We've almost finished the project! The only ethical thing to do is to try to find more funding. People are counting on me—"

—And who does he think we are? What does he think we've been doing? We've been counting on him!

"I feel terrible. I do. I know this is really hard for you guys to understand. I promise I will make it up to you."

Dad goes on. "Just know that we're helping five new clinics get built! Think of all the good that's going to put in the world! It's a crime how long these people have been waiting for decent health care and educational facilities. We're providing that!"

Finally, he has nothing left to say, and it's clear Cal and I are upset. So Mom says good-bye for all of us and hangs up. Then she turns to us and pastes on a sad smile. "I know you boys are disappointed. I know you miss him. But let's try to remember the bigger picture. Your dad's saving lives! He's a superhero!"

A superhero.

I bet John Lockdown wouldn't leave his own kids, even if it meant saving a whole village. Or would he?

I don't know what else to do so I go wait in the car for Mom to drive us to school. I sit in back and pretend to rummage through my backpack for the whole entire ride—so they won't see me trying to hide my stupid tears.

18

THAT AFTERNOON, I'm doing math homework in my room when something totally strange and unusual happens. My phone . . . actually . . . buzzes.

It's not Mom. And it's not Joon. It's a text. From Liberty Silverberg.

Lib: So? How were Uncle Dan's comics?

Stan: Good! Thanks again. Really cool stuff.

Lib: Come on, that Archie one wasn't cool.

Stan: Archie's cool!

I laugh and go back to math. Graphs. Slopes. Points to plot. If x, then y. I wish everything were as straightforward as math. If this specific x happens, then this specific y will exactly follow. That's so reassuring.

But life is not like math. Life is more like: If x, then . . . WHY?

About three pieces of graph paper later, Mom knocks at my door. Her smile seems a bit dangerously wide.

"Hey, kiddo. I was just talking to Dr. Silverberg."

"Um, okay?"

"Liberty told him you two are getting to be friends, and that you liked those old vintage comics of his. Then she told him about this Trivia Quest contest of yours. And so then he thought—and I thought—we all thought: Well, my goodness! Wouldn't it be fun for you two to enter together?"

I can't believe my ears. "Are you kidding me?"

"I kid you not!" Mom looks giddy with triumph. "It's a great idea! You both need to get out more. Fresh air, and fun, and a new challenge. It's a perfect activity for you both! Right? Am I right or am I right?"

My mouth can't quite form any words. The entry form I was going to ask Mom to sign—the solo entry form—is still sitting right here on my desk.

Mom continues. "You love comic trivia; she wants a chance to get out more and explore. Perfect! Right?" She tilts her head and smiles. "Her mother is very protective, but Dr. Dan thinks he can talk her into it."

Heat rises to my face; my chest goes squirmy.

"She's been through a lot, that girl. Her uncle wants her to have a nice new start."

I frown and shut my math book. "What exactly is it that Liberty's been through, Mom? What's the big secret going on?" I ask.

Mom's dangerously wide smile shrinks a little bit. "I'm sure they'll tell us when they're ready."

19

LISTEN. I KNOW they forced us," says Liberty Silverberg, glancing at me while fidgeting in my desk chair. "But still. It could be an okay time. " She swivels the chair back and forth and back and forth, trying to make it squeak. "I'm good with hanging out downtown for a day, and, hey, you can geek out about comics. What's not to love. Right?"

"There's a lot more to winning this serious and important contest than hanging out and geeking out, Liberty," I say.

"I know. Didn't mean to minimize all your amazing trivia knowledge." She rolls her eyes.

"Okay, then," I say.

"My mom's not too happy about me doing this, which

105

is an added bonus! She's so overprotective, I want to scream!" Liberty scrunches up her face and wags her finger. "'Liberty,'" she mimics, "'How are you feeling? Liberty, please check in!' She makes me text her three times a day!" She spins in the chair, around and around.

"Why's she so overprotective, Liberty?"

Liberty lets the chair come to a stop. She sticks her long thin legs straight out in front of her, and considers her dirty purple sneakers. "I was kind of sick a while back. That's all."

"And?"

"And nothing. Hey. There are better reasons to do the Trivia Quest than ticking off my mom. I mean, this is your chance to shine, Stanley." Liberty grins. "Comic trivia is your superpower! And I bring complementary skills. I can find my way around, look people in the eye, and actually talk to them! I'll help you out, dude. We'll be a team."

I don't know whether to feel glad or ashamed. So I open a map. We go over some of the downtown landmarks, figure out where the convention center is, and Balboa Park. Biggest park in the nation, home to a ton of museums and the San Diego Zoo.

"And here's the ballpark. And the civic theatre. Here's the harbor," I tell her. "Cruise ships, Maritime Museum, boats. And here? This is Waterfront Park. Fountains, grass, food trucks."

"Yeah, food trucks, yum," she says. "Uncle Dan and I were down there last week. The sushi one. Sub Diego. Phil's BBQ . . . Hey, can we stop for lunch?"

Great. The Trivia Quest is next Saturday, and Liberty's commitment to studying is as bad as Joon's.

We head downstairs and Liberty says, "You know, not to scare you or anything, but I did happen to notice there's a ton of people entering this thing. So, just prepare yourself."

I stop in my tracks. "How big?"

"Oh, hundreds of contestants."

I grip the banister tightly. All my muscles tense. "I don't do well in crowds."

"I know. Not to worry," she says. "I'll be with you." She punches my shoulder, joking, and I notice again how bony and flimsy her wrist is. The skin almost see-through, with faint blue veins like branches of some dead tree.

A worry-tree.

All week long, I'm doing the single-digit countdown to Saturday and the Trivia Quest with an ice-storm of dread in my gut. It's looming like a gallows at the end of a dark tunnel. Like a nameless nightmare of fear.

The only good thing about this week, is at least Principal

Coffin hasn't inflicted any safety drills on us.

At lunch on Friday, Joon and Dylan are telling everyone how cool it's going to be at the Quest tomorrow. How they're soooo going to win it.

I don't say a word. I'm sitting down at the end, not saying anything at all, as usual. Nobody knows I've entered. Not even Joon.

"So the clues are all over downtown?" Keefner asks Dylan, munching that same disgusting bologna, ketchup, and pickle sandwich he brings every day.

"Yeah," Dylan says. "Seven clues. Joon and I have it covered. We'll know where to go."

Joon nods, but I think I see a flashing glimpse of deer-in-the-headlights in his brown eyes.

"I heard that when they held the New York version they ran out of gold tokens and people rioted," says Keefner. "Total mob scene."

Wait, what? I freeze.

"Yeah," Keefner goes on. "People go nuts at these events. Some guys in New York got trampled and ended up in the hospital."

Is that true? I don't say anything. Just try to push down my Red Alerts.

Dylan scowls at Keefner. "Don't worry! We can handle it."

I have a feeling Joon's staring at me, but I keep my head down—until I hear Dylan's voice mocking: "Hey, Fart-in-bra! Trivia king! You entering, too?"

The whole table laughs so hard they don't even see me nod, minutely, yes.

Then I start to get mad. I think of what Liberty would say. What John Lockdown would do. I grip the sides of the bench as hard as I can. "Yes," I say, as calmly and loudly as I can.

Keefner and Dylan just keep laughing at me. But Joon's eyes widen.

"YES!" I shout.

The chatter around me stops.

Then Keefner starts chuckling. "Oh, great! If someone's gonna end up getting trampled in the mob tomorrow, three to one it'll be Fart-in-bra here!" he says. And everyone starts talking again.

I try to pretend I didn't hear. But inside I think: Keefner's probably right.

20

TIME FOR THE Heart Health and Defibrillator Use Assembly!" blares Principal Coffin's static-scratchy voice. "Would everyone please report to the auditorium?"

It figures.

I veer into the main office.

Mrs. Ngozo is by the teachers' mailboxes. "Your mother tells me you're competing in that big comics festival competition, tomorrow, Stanley," she says as I walk past. "That's amazing! We're very proud of you. Just getting out there and participating in something you care about, that makes you a winner in my book!" She gives me two thumbs-up. "And don't forget to breathe, Stanley! Aqua, ochre!"

"Thanks, Mrs. Ngozo," I say. And head quickly past

her to the Ready Room.

The last comic from the mystery artist showed John Lockdown vanquishing the big dumb bully, then telling me that somehow, someday, my super-senses would turn to superpowers.

Ha.

I take a black marker and write in thick letters:

Although actually, I'd just be happy to get through it alive.

"You look pale," Mom says during dinner that night. She puts her hand on my forehead. "Try to eat—you'll need your energy tomorrow!"

"Yeah, Stannie," says Cal, sneering. "Listen to your mommy!"

Mom ignores him. "I talked to your father again," she says. "He's sad to miss Stanley's big contest!" She piles a heaping mass of potatoes onto my plate. "He would have loved to have been around to cheer you on."

"I think you should stop making excuses for Dad, already," I say. "Here's not here. He's not here to cheer me on. Okay?"

My stomach's a knot, so I ask to be excused. I head up to my room, launch myself onto my bed. Why am I even doing this Trivia Quest? I could . . . get lost get mugged melt down overload feel scared lose Liberty lose the contest lose my way . . .

I pull out my phone.

Stan: Maybe we should just bag it tomorrow. I'm thinking it's probably going to be way too hard for me.

Lib: Be in our driveway by 8:15. OR ELSE.

112

Okay, I give up. I sigh, and turn out the light.

Yip! Yip! AwOOOOO!!! The eerie noises start in the back of my head, then build louder and louder, until . . . I bolt upright and peer out my window. In dim moonlight, I count one, two, three, four coyotes. Their shadows slip and weave around a small dark lump in the grass.

Across the hall, I hear Cal's bed creak. A moment later he opens my door, rubbing his eyes. "They're at it again, huh?" he whispers.

"Yup," I say. "They've got something."

Cal practically falls on me while tugging open my window. Then he sticks his head out and screams loud enough to wake half the town: "YAHHH! GIT! GIT!"

A few sets of glinting yellow eyes turn toward us for a frozen moment. Cal is hanging so far out the windowsill, I have to hold onto his legs. "YAHH! YAHH!"

One coyote, twice the size of the rest, stares up at us while the rest slink off down the canyon slope. Then he slowly follows as Cal pretends to aim an invisible rifle at him.

Meanwhile, the small dark lump is still in the grass.

"What is that, Cal? Does it need help?" It's hard to catch my breath and talk right.

He shrugs. "Just a rabbit," Cal says, already on his way

back to his room. "Probably died of fright. Fear alone can kill rabbits, you know."

I imagine what that would feel like: your heart thumping in such a panic-frenzy, it actually seizes up and stops.

It seems like moments later when Mom knocks at my door. But the sun is bright. Birds are chirping.

"Stanley?" She peeks her head in. "It's late! Time to get going!"

I groan and pull the blankets over my head.

She comes over and peels them back. "Let's take it step by step," she says. "Just wash up and come downstairs. That's all you have to do. We'll take it from there."

Before I get up, I check the yard through the window. The dead rabbit is gone. Or it was a dream.

When I come downstairs, Mom's in the kitchen in her bathrobe, scrambling eggs and talking on the phone. Albert Einstein is sprawled over her feet so she has to shuffle around him. He lifts his head, thumps his tail, and rubs the drool off his flubber-lips onto my pant leg as Mom hands me the phone.

"Stan?" It's Dad.

"Where are you?"

"Nairobi airport."

"Does that mean you're coming home?"

"No, no, no. I'm picking up a late supply shipment. I

just—well. Your mother told me what you're doing today, and I wanted to say I'm proud of you! You're getting out of the house, doing stuff. That's great!"

I glare at Mom, who's concentrating hard on scrambling eggs.

"I'm sure you'll do great. I'm proud of you! And I love you."

Something inside me loosens toward Dad. Just a little. A small nudge of loosening. "Okay thanks," I murmur, and hand the phone to Mom in exchange for a plate of eggs.

"You'd better get a move on," she says. "Mrs. Lee mentioned to me the other day that Joon was entering, too—I told Dr. Dan so you could all carpool. He's driving the whole lot of you. And Mrs. Lee's picking up." She looks at her watch. "I've got to get to work, kiddo. Time for you to go."

I freeze. "Joon?" I finally stutter. "In the same car?"

She stops and gives me her patented laser-beam Look. "What's wrong with that, Stanley?" she says.

"Nothing," I mumble, grabbing my backpack and heading out the door.

Honestly. Mothers.

22

DR. SILVERBERG and Liberty are already sitting in their car, idling out in front of their house. Dr. Silverberg is so tall his head hits the car ceiling. I hop in back and mutter my good mornings, and through the front windshield, we watch Joon and Dylan walking down the street toward us.

Which means Dylan probably slept over Joon's. I used to do that, in some other life.

"You'll have to squeeze in—sorry about the leg room back there," says Dr. Silverberg. "It's Joon, is it? And Dylan? Glad to meet you! Glad we could carpool!"

That makes one of us.

Dylan takes the hump, blocking Joon completely from my sight. Not that I want to see him.

"Isn't this an exciting day?" Dr. Silverberg goes on, in total hyper-enthusiasm mode, as he pulls out onto the road. "Comic book trivia! I used to love comics when I was your age!"

"It's gonna be awesome! A whole day to hang out downtown!" Dylan says, nodding and leaning forward.

Liberty turns to stare at him coolly. "Oh! Is this just about hanging out downtown?" she says with an evil grin. "I thought it was about competing to win those VIP badges to Comic Fest. I know I'm feeling pretty lucky Stanley's on my team!" Then she winks at me.

I can feel blood rush suddenly into my face.

But Dylan isn't offended or anything. He laughs, then claps once, loudly. His elbows and knees are every-where—he's taking up more than half the backseat. "Are you throwing down a challenge? Seriously? It's ON! You two, prepare to be totally destroyed." Then he and Joon slap five, laughing.

Breathe, I tell myself. Breathe, breathe. Aqua. Ochre.

I pretend to be fascinated by the scenery of dry brown hills, buildings, glimpses of ocean, and traffic. The high-way ticks by under the car wheels. Joon and Dylan talk about soccer and football and a party someone is throw-ing in a few weeks. Liberty and her uncle pretty much ride in silence. And all too soon, outside the window, the city skyline looms.

I imagine John Lockdown flying between those shiny buildings, surveying over the harbor, keeping watch on this Quest. Keeping watch over me.

If only.

23

THE GREAT San Diego Comic Trivia Quest! Best Quest *in the West!*

That's what the gold banner at the drop-off point says. It snaps in the wind above the plaza, and behind it, the convention center rises like a crazy spaceship of glass and concrete.

Bright red trolley cars whir past. Cars honk. People are everywhere, crossing the street on their way to the plaza.

This is it. We're here.

I'm so nervous, my teeth are chattering.

"See that sign? Mrs. Lee will pick you up right on that corner," says Dr. Silverberg. "Stay in touch with us, okay? Liberty? Call and check in. Your mom insists you call or text her every hour, on the hour today. You hear me?"

Liberty groans and pretends to faint.

"Have fun! Good luck!" Dr. Silverberg seems almost as nervous as me. Then he veers over to the curb—and suddenly, we're dumped out on the sidewalk, and his car is swallowed up by the traffic. Gone.

People, noise, heat, exhaust—it hits me at once. A jolt. My heart pounds. My knees go wobbly. My skin crawls.

Liberty looks me straight in the eye. "You okay?"

I'm not sure I am, but I nod anyway. And we follow Joon and Dylan into the plaza.

People are everywhere. The air is thick with the smell of deodorant and sunscreen. And even though the Quest instructions said no costumes, I spot some cosplayers: Deadpools, Ant-Men, Yodas, Harley Quinns.

Liberty points to a group of them. "Those people are hard-core."

Dylan says, "Yeah! Those are real fans. Not like us. We probably won't make it past the first clue."

"Speak for yourself," Liberty sneers. "And don't forget Stan's like the comic trivia overlord of the century."

"Hardly anyone will win passes," Joon says. "It's supposed to be really hard."

"Well, *we're* going to," Liberty snaps back.

"Stop it," I whisper, holding my ears.

The last thing I need right now is their trash talk.

We head into separate lines for registration. The officials check our paperwork, then hand us contestant badges, as well as this little blue plastic brick with an LED screen on the front. It fits in the palm of Liberty's hand.

"This is called a pager," the registration guy says. "In a little while, your starting clue will scroll onto that little screen. The Quest committee came up with about twenty different starting clues so everyone doesn't go to the same place at once. Anyhow, just hold on to this, and get ready to start!"

Liberty herds me through to the central platform like a crowd-parting machine. "Come on, Stanley! Let's go!" Her grip on my wrist is like an iron birdclaw. I look around, trying to locate Joon and Dylan, but we've lost them.

As we weave through the horde, I try to squash down my flashes of crowd-panic. I try to remember I'm not a little lost kid. I'm in control. I can do this. I think of Dad's words. I think of Mrs. Ngozo, and aqua, and ochre. And I imagine John Lockdown, standing on top of the convention center, hands on hips, cape flying. Watching over me, making sure I'm okay.

By the time Liberty finds a spot she likes, the opening music is starting.

GONGGGGG!

The crowd comes to a standstill. Up on the platform, a black-caped figure in a gold mask steps up. He raises the sides of his cloak, Dracula-style, then turns around so we can see that across the back, in gold lettering, it says: *THE MASTER*. There's wild cheering as he turns again to face us.

"Greetings, Questers!" The familiar, deep voice booms through the sound system and vibrates in my jumpy gut. "What a most MARVEL-ous day!"

People go wild, cheering and clapping. I cover my ears to dampen the onslaught of noise, and look around for Joon. His idol! He must be going nuts. If only I were standing with him! Liberty's clearly never even heard of the Master. She stands with her arms crossed, impatient and unimpressed.

"It's 10:00 a.m. You have seven hours to solve seven clues and capture seven gold coins. In a few moments, your pagers will start to buzz with your very first clue. Because there are several hundred of you, we've taken a few measures to make the Quest run smoothly, so listen carefully." The plaza goes completely silent.

"Note that the clues are of equal difficulty, but different. So don't follow your competitors. Your goal is to solve the clues you get. March to your own drummer; don't worry about anybody else.

"And a note on transportation. Nothing is much farther than a twenty- or twenty-five-minute walk. But your Trivia Quest contestant badges allow you free access to the downtown bus and trolley system. So don't lose them!"

People are quiet now, listening.

"And I'd advise you to keep a low profile as you approach a clue locale. You don't want to tip off other contestants, or accidentally reveal anything to them. This means certain ones among you may want to consider removing your somewhat conspicuous Yoda heads."

The crowd laughs.

"If you think you've solved a clue and are in the right location, open your eyes and look around. A Trivia Quest official, who may or may not be disguised as a comic book 'character,' should be nearby. Find them and tell them the correct answer, and you'll receive one of these." The Master holds up a gold coin about the size of a poker chip. "Collect seven of these, bring them back here by 5:00 p.m. tonight, and you'll earn VIP passes to Comic Fest. Earn less than seven, and we still have some nifty consolation prizes for you.

"Now," the Master continues in his deep, mysterious voice, "with no further ado . . ."

A long drumroll thunders from the speakers while everyone stares, transfixed, at their little plastic pagers. My heart thumps. Liberty's hand is actually shaking as she holds our pager tight, her thumbnail white with pressure.

"Don't hold it so tight," I tell her. "You'll crack it or something!"

BEEEEEP! The speakers pulse out the starting sound—to match the Red Alerts now pulsing through my body—and the pager in Liberty's hand finally vibrates.

Then, she drops it.

24

PEOPLE ARE SCRAMBLING away in every direction. Legs, feet, stomping all around us. "Pick it up! Get our pager! Before someone steps on it!" I scream. I am going to have a heart attack, and we haven't even gotten our first clue.

"I don't see it!" she shouts. "Where is it?"

We scramble, darting this way and that. It was blue—I look for blue. Is that it? No! That's someone's sneaker.

Then a flash of blue plastic pops into sight to my left. I dash between the hairy legs of a big man—right before he lowers his shoe onto our pager, I grab it, scraping my knuckles on the cement.

"Watch it, kid!" says the guy, veering off.

The plaza has practically emptied by the time Liberty

125

and I hold up our scratched blue plastic pager, trembling, and stare at the little screen.

The first part of the clue has already scrolled past! The remainder pops up now . . .

To a certain location . . . Where information . . . Is a-'hoardin' . . .

We look at each other in disbelief. I scream, "We've missed it! We've lost already!"

"No we haven't! It's still scrolling!" shouts Liberty.

. . . By someone name of Gordon.

That's ridiculous. Information. Hoardin'. Gordon.

Wait. That's not ridiculous.

A surge of relief washes through me.

I grab Liberty's hand. Her bulging green eyes are almost as full of stress as mine.

"What is it, Stanley?"

"Someone name of Gordon."

Her face goes blank.

"Seriously? Haven't you ever even seen a Batman movie?"

A light sparks in her eyes. "Oh, the police guy? Commissioner Gordon?"

"Yes! Batman's ally in the fight against the criminals of Gotham. So what's Commissioner Gordon's *location, where information is a-hoardin'*?" I prompt her.

My heart's beating hard now, but it's not with nervousness. It's with excitement.

"Um, that would be . . . a police headquarters?"

I smile.

"So where do we go?"

"You're the one in charge of the directions," I say.

She pulls out a laminated pocket map of the city from her backpack and thinks for a minute. "That way!"

Up the hill we go, over the trolley tracks, past little shops and businesses, along the busy sidewalk. We wait at a ridiculously long red light. There's a bunch of other Questers standing there, waiting to cross.

"The police station is that way, I think!" Liberty says, pushing at me to go left.

"SSSH!" I say. "Remember what the Master said? Don't talk so loud!" A few Questers overhear us and laugh.

"Don't worry, kid." A tattooed guy with a long brown beard elbows me, showing me a green pager just like our blue one. "My clue's got me headed somewhere different right now. But I'll file that police-station hint in case I need it later!"

I smile and nod. But inside, I start to crumble a little. "Don't give away our clue information, okay?" I hiss at Liberty as the light turns green.

127

"Sorry," Liberty says as she skips ahead of me across the street. "I just got a little excited! I'll control myself." She smiles back at me. "Downtown's fun! This is gonna be fun!"

As for me, I'm fighting nausea. "Wait!" I call as we hit the other side of the street. I lean against the corner building. I have to get control over my sensory overload.

Traffic horns. Exhaust. Glaring sunlight. Bodies pushing past. It's a lot for me. No one gets this—my mom, my brother, Dad, Gramps, Joon—no one in my life has ever gotten this. How the whole world sometimes feels like it comes crashing down on my head. How everything's suddenly too much.

I don't expect Liberty to get it. But at least she's sticking nearby, looking concerned. "You okay?"

I take a deep breath and nod. "Just let's stand here a minute, okay?"

I lean against the building and close my eyes, trying to summon John Lockdown in my head. John Lockdown is impervious to noise. He does epic battle with sensory assault. He is fearless. What would he tell me to do now?

As I open my eyes, a sudden giant gust of wind swirls up street dust and makes me turn away—and I notice something down the side street. A strange building. I've seen photos of it before—modern, with a giant woven-metal globe stuck into it. It's the kind of building you could imagine appearing in a comic.

Is that what John Lockdown would tell me to do? Go there?

Suddenly, it hits me. I know what that building is.

"Change of plans, Liberty," I say, finally breathing normally again. "We're going to the library."

25

THE CENTRAL LIBRARY is a big, wide-open space, but it's quickly filling up with people—they're streaming in, grabbing tables and chairs, spreading out into the stacks of books to browse. Everyone seems to know exactly what they're doing here, and where they're going. Except us.

"Where should we look?" Liberty asks. "And what are we looking FOR?"

"Shh!" I say, looking around. "I don't think that clue is about Commissioner Gordon. It's about his daughter."

"And who's that?"

"*Barbara* Gordon. Batgirl."

"Aha! Oookay. And . . . ?"

"She runs Gotham City Public Library. Barbara Gordon is a computer whiz who does a lot of research and detective work. She's like the queen of data security for Batman." I could go on and on with Batgirl factoids, but I check myself.

"Seems to me it could equally be the police station. The police hoard their information, too."

"Well, yeah, but that's so obvious. Let's check this place out quickly, and if the answer's not really Batgirl, we'll try the police station. Deal?"

We head up to the first level. "So what's this Barbara Gordon look like, anyway?" Liberty asks.

"It depends on what comic you're reading, but she's pretty much always got red hair and glasses."

"Then let's go scope out the employees. You heard what the Master said about Quest officials in costume. Maybe she's pretending to be a librarian."

We do a methodic sweep, every area, floor by floor, but there are no red-haired, eye-glassed librarians in sight. Then, in desperation, we go back through and check name tags. None of them read *Gordon*.

"Nothing seems out of the ordinary about this library, Stanley. It's all business as usual. Are you sure this is right? Maybe we should ask someone," Liberty says, frowning. "And don't forget the time. If we still come up empty, we'll have to go to the police station. Quick."

We head over to the information desk where an old librarian guy with a long gray ponytail sits reading.

"Hey, um, excuse me," Liberty says. "Can you tell us where books and info about comics are located?"

He taps on his keyboard in a way that's slower than humanly possible: one key every five seconds. Then he reaches for a pencil and carefully prints a number on a little card for us. I'm jumping up and down by the time that pencil starts forming the last number because we've already wasted too much time.

"Is there some meaning to that number? Do you think it's a code or something?" Liberty says, frowning.

"I don't know. Let's check the stacks." We wander until we find the right section.

"Here's comics," Liberty says. "But there's no book or comic that's just about Batgirl, or Barbara Gordon. Or hoarding information."

The whirring motor of anxiety in my chest is starting to speed up. "We're wasting time!" I hiss.

"I think we should have gone to the police station. This is wrong, Stan."

I have to swallow hard and give myself a moment before I can finally admit defeat. "Okay." I sigh. "Let's try the police station now."

We silently make our way toward the entrance. I'm miserable over how much time we've taken—we're still on the first clue, and it's already after eleven o'clock. This Trivia Quest is going to be even harder than I thought.

It's a big city—if all the clues are this vague, we'll never get seven coins.

Before we exit the library, Liberty stops to take a sip at the drinking fountain. While I wait for her, tapping my toe, I notice something: a flyer, pasted right above the fountain, printed with the following words:

SPECIAL EXHIBIT:
THE ART OF THE COMIC
ART GALLERY, TOP FLOOR

As Robin once said in the old 1960s Batman TV series: *"Holy Crucial Moment, Batman!"*

26

WE BURST OUT of the elevator at the rooftop level, and Liberty rushes to the edge. "Wow! Check out the view!" she says. "You can see all of San Diego! And look at the ocean!"

"Get back!" I yank at the hem of her shirt. "Watch out!"

She looks at me carefully. "Don't you like the ocean?"

"We need to find Barbara Gordon, not sightsee," I say.

The gallery is pretty much right behind us. A metal door is propped open—taped on it is another sign that reads: *The Art of the Comic.* We tiptoe in. And:

Bingo!

Inside, the walls are covered with vintage comics,

both originals and prints. Some are blown up really huge-sized. I love the look of those pixilated little dots. Crowded together, the dots look like solid color on the old, pulpy pages. Spread the dots apart, and the shading gets really light. Those ink dots are like the comic's atoms, the basic building blocks of comic art.

"Whoa." I rush over to a panel with a hooded figure in a familiar green cloak. It's Joon's old favorite, the Green Lama, in an original print from the 1940s!

"Man, I wish Joon were here," I say.

Liberty comes and stands by me. She doesn't say anything—just punches me on the shoulder.

"No offense," I add.

"None taken," she says.

We notice a pad of crude sketches for something called *Beetle Bailey*. "Hey," she says, "is this place making you think about your giant Sketchpad of Mystery, or whatever you call it? Maybe that John Lockdown artist is somewhere nearby, doing the Trivia Quest today, too."

I smile. Then, suddenly, I feel a gentle tap on my elbow.

A lady has rolled up to us in her wheelchair. She has short red hair, heavy black-framed glasses, and a strange smile on her face.

"Excuse me," she says, looking around suspiciously. "I'm glad you're enjoying the exhibit. But I have to say . . .

Did I just happen to hear you mention . . . something?"

Liberty starts jumping up and down like she's on a trampoline.

I swallow hard. "Yes! We're on the Trivia Quest. We're looking for—well—for you, I think! Are you Barbara Gordon? Who *hoards information*, at a library *location*, for a certain Caped Crusader?"

"Named Batman!" says Liberty, doing a little dance. I roll my eyes.

The lady in the wheelchair smiles. "Congratulations, kids!" She glances around. "Let's keep our voices down. Half the fun is letting the other contestants figure it out for themselves. Also, the Quest team requests that you *do not* share answers to clues. Promise?"

We both hold up our hands and swear. We're grinning from ear to ear.

"You can leave me your pager," she says quietly, putting out her hand.

Liberty can barely fish it out of her pocket, she's so excited. Then, "Barbara Gordon" reaches into a little cloth tote bag attached to the side of her wheelchair, and pulls out a shiny golden coin with a big letter *Q* embossed on it.

"Here is your token—don't lose it." She hands it to Liberty, who zips it into her backpack.

"And here's your next clue," the lady adds, handing

me a tiny unmarked envelope the size of a business card, made of stiff gold paper. "Don't read it until you're far enough away from me to be inconspicuous."

We can barely contain ourselves in the crowded elevator, heading back out. We try to walk casually and slowly. But by the time we're on the street again, we're jumping up and down.

"One down!" I shout.

"Six to go!" Liberty shouts back. She looks down at me carefully. "You good?"

I nod. I'm jittery and excited, but I'm good. So far, so good.

We sit on a bench, and I try to chill out. But my hands are shaking as I remove the small, mysterious card from its golden envelope.

> *I was twenty-nine and still striking*
> *When this old hero put on the first comic mask.*
> *My hands still work. But where am I now?*
> *That's what you need to ask.*

27

"I WAS TWENTY–NINE and still striking when this old *hero put on the first comic mask* . . . ?" Liberty stares hard at the paper. "'Still striking' is what you say about old people when they still look attractive. That they're 'still striking.'" She sighs. "And who was the first superhero to put on a mask? Superman? Was Lois Lane supposed to be a striking twenty-nine-year-old or something?"

I smile. "Superman was early, but he wasn't the first costumed superhero. Come on! You should know this— there was a Clock comic in the stack you lent me from your uncle's moving boxes."

Her eyebrows shoot up. "You're kidding me."

"I kid you not," I say. "*He* was the first masked super-hero—mid 1930s. Predates Superman. The Clock was a lawyer by day, and wore a regular, old-fashioned suit and hat with his mask. And when he'd solved a crime or knocked out a bad guy, he left a calling card that said *The Clock Has Struck*."

"The clock has struck . . . So, a striking clock. A clock that's still striking?" Liberty says, slowly, thinking it through. "But what about the next two lines? *My hands still work. But where am I now? That's what you need to ask?*"

"Definitely sounds like they mean a *real* clock." I start to breathe quicker. "An old clock that's still working. That's maybe located somewhere around here."

"Okay. So. A clock that was twenty-nine years old, back in the mid 1930s—a clock that was built around 1900 or so."

We head back to the library information desk. The super-slow gray-ponytailed librarian is right where we left him.

"YOU talk to him," I say, nudging Liberty.

She rolls her eyes but she steps forward. "Sir? We're looking for local information," Liberty says. "Do you know anything about a sort of old clock somewhere within walking distance of here? Something built around 1900?"

He slowly, slowly reaches his hand down behind the desk and brings up a rubber-banded stack of tourist brochures. "Well . . . yeah . . ." He thumbs slowly through them, and finally hands one over.

It says *Welcome to Horton Plaza* on the cover. I think my mom's gone shopping there before. Yes. It's a downtown shopping complex. "There's . . . an old clock . . . somewhere . . . in that plaza . . . ," says the super-slow librarian. "Is that . . . what you mean?"

"That is *so* what we mean," says Liberty breathlessly. We thank him, and we're off, sprinting toward Horton Plaza as fast as we can.

28

LIBERTY SHOULD BE on a track team with those stork legs. My right side is one big knotted-up cramp.

"Slow down!" I yell.

"Keep up!" she yells back.

Finally, a sign for the entrance to Horton Plaza appears. We dash into a maze of walkways at odd angles, past fancy department stores and water fountains and kiosks and escalators and shops.

"The clock should be over . . . there!" Liberty shouts, and we keep running and dodging this way and that, poking down walkways, until:

There it is, in the center of a little plaza. A beautiful old clock, up high on a pole, with lacy metal designs. It looks hundreds of years old—and totally out of place in front of all the modern window displays.

We slow way down before we approach it. Now we need to act cool so we don't tip off any other Questers.

The clock is like something out of a European fairy tale. It has a big, white face that says "Correct Time, San Diego," in old-fashioned lettering. All around the perimeter are smaller clock faces that tell the time all over the world.

It makes me think of Dad in Africa. It's 11:30 a.m. here now—late at night for him. "I'm sure you'll do great," he had said to me this morning on the phone. Yeah, well, so far I'm not doing so great. It took us forever to get through that first clue. At this rate, we'll never make it through all seven.

I try to get my breathing under control and stop panting like a dog. I spy a bench—we slide onto it, and Liberty tries to casually open the brochure, like we're just your average Macy's shoppers.

"Okay. So. Yeah. So this thing is called the Jessop's Street Clock. It was built for a downtown San Diego jeweler back in 1907," she reads to me. We stare at the old, grainy photo of the exact same clock, back more than one hundred years ago, with a horse and buggy by it. "It was relocated here when Horton Plaza was built. A famous local landmark."

I do the math quickly in my head. "So, if I'm

remembering right that the comic called the Clock first 'struck' in, say, around 1936 . . . Subtract twenty-nine years from that, and what do you get?"

"You get 1907!" she says. Liberty's watery green eyes are glowing.

My chest swells with pride. "This clock was twenty-nine years old, already—and *still striking* on Jessop Street—when the Clock comic was first created! We got this one!"

We sit for a minute, looking at each other.

"Okay, so?" she finally says. "We solved it. What do we do now? Where's the person? The contact?"

We look around, bewildered, but there's no one tapping us on the shoulder like Barbara Gordon did at the library. No one who looks Clock—or officially Quest—related.

Some other shoppers—or maybe fellow Questers—are starting to stroll and linger . . . Two guys in Batman T-shirts are lurking by the front doors of Macy's. Suspicious, to say the least.

"Let's walk around," Liberty says, getting up off the bench.

I try to remember everything I can about the Clock's alter ego. A lawyer or cop, or something. With an Irish name. McBride? McBrian? O'Brian?

There's a group of mothers with baby strollers

power-walking past. The two Quester dudes are still whispering by Macy's. A homeless person, wrapped in thick layers of rags and a dirty down vest, shuffles around a corner. He looks so out of place among all the stores. It's sad. But everyone pretends not to notice him. If this were a real comic strip, the homeless man might turn out to be Rorschach in disguise. Or maybe John Lockdown on undercover assignment.

A group of fancy older ladies push through the doors to Macy's, bumping the two suspicious-looking Quester dudes. More people arrive . . . I scan them for signs of an old-fashioned lawyer named O'Brian. Or anything clock-related. But: nothing.

There's a coffee hut across the plaza from the clock. On the awning, it says *Java Time*. And there's a picture of a coffee cup with a big clock on it.

Hmm. Liberty and I look at each other. "*Time* for java?" she says.

We head over, and she steps right up and orders: "Two small regular coffees!"

"Coffee? Really?" I say.

"Yup. My mom won't let me drink it," she says, waving a handful of sugar packets. "But she's not here, is she."

"Two regulars." The coffee guy turns around to face us, holding two small white cups.

He's got on an old hat with a brim. Under his green

barista apron he's wearing a three-piece business suit, one with big wide shoulders, like they used to wear in those old gangster movies my dad likes to watch.

I take a sharp breath and hold it.

Yup.

His name tag says *Brian O'Brien.*

Liberty is looking at me, eyebrows raised. I nudge her. She nudges me back. Finally, I get her to step forward and ask the question.

"Hello. I guess my friend here—or teammate, I should say—is kind of shy. But he thinks you might be the Clock guy?" she says. "Something to do with the Clock? Trivia Quest?" She gives him a brilliant smile and looks at me for approval.

It's not enough detail. I'm going to have to speak up, myself. Heart pounding, I lean over the counter and add, in a whisper: "The big old clock over there, it was *twenty-nine—and still striking*— when the Clock comic book character was created, back in the 1930s. The old character of the Clock, the first masked comic book hero? Is that it?"

The undercover barista wipes his hands on a piece of black cloth and whistles softly. "Verrrry good!" His eyes dart suspiciously this way and that. "I'm not supposed to talk too much to you Questers, but let me just say congratulations. This clue was a tough one."

My chest swells and tightens with excitement.

Brian ducks behind the counter. "Here's your change, sir," he says, handing me our second golden token of the day. "And here's your *receipt*." Then he steps back into the shadow.

We walk away from the coffee hut, sneak off around the corner to find a quiet spot where we can check out that *receipt*.

Which is not a receipt at all, of course. It's the little gold envelope with the next clue.

29

There's a certain black boat
and a superhero dame
Called one and the same—
Natasha's other name.
That's where you need to go.
You'll find it down below.

"How are your super-senses, Stanley?" Liberty asks me when we're seated on the bench. It's almost noon, and she's just texted her mom *"not dead yet"* for like the sixth time this morning. She gulps her coffee and smacks her lips. "Are you hanging in there, Stan? You know, you gotta learn to speak up to people. They won't bite your head off."

I make a face at her. "I thought the speaking was your

part of the bargain. I solve the clues, you're the public interface."

"Yeah, well . . . I'm just saying."

We sit in silence for a moment, thinking. She finishes her coffee, so I hand her my cup, and she keeps sipping. "Okay," she finally says. "So tell me about this next one, genius. Who's Natasha?"

I sigh. "Liberty, haven't you seen any Avengers movies? Natasha is the, the . . ."

Out of the corner of my eye, I notice those two guys in Batman T-shirts walking near. They grab the bench next to us.

We smile; they smile. We are clutching a clue; they are clutching a clue.

I whisper to Liberty: "Let's move somewhere else." We get up but one of the men raises his hand and shouts, "Hey! Kids! Hang on a minute!"

Liberty stops cold, and I walk right into her.

"Do we detect fellow Questers?" the man calls out.

Woop.

Okay, that's a Red Alert.

"Um, we're not supposed to talk to strangers. Come on, Liberty!" I say.

But Liberty's stopped in her tracks, clutching our Natasha clue. I can practically see wheels turning in her brain. "Wait a second, Stan," she says. "Let's hear what he has to say."

"Liberty!" I hiss. "That's cheating!"

The guy says, "We figured out the Clock clue, just like you guys, but if you hadn't led us to the coffee hut, I don't know if we would've put that together."

"Yeah, thanks," the second guy adds. "And we were thinking. How about we team up for a bit? Or at least do some information sharing?"

Guy One leans in. "What clue did you get?"

"That's cheating," I say, staring at the ground, my heart starting to pound. I was doing so well until now— had almost forgotten to be nervous.

"What's the harm?" says Guy One, waving his small envelope. "Don't you want to know what we know?"

The question hangs in the air for a heavy second. "No dice," I finally say. "Cheating ruins winning."

"The point here's to get us all VIP passes," says Guy Two.

"But cheating takes the meaning out of it. It takes all the fun out of it."

"Yeah!" Liberty adds.

I want to get away from those guys so I take off, winding my way out of Horton Plaza. I only hope Liberty is still behind me.

At the crosswalk, Liberty taps me on the shoulder. "Did you mean it? What you said?"

"About what?"

"That cheating would take the fun out of it?"

I nod.

"Well, then, that's big. You know what that means, don't you? It means that in spite of how stressed you look right now, you think there's something *fun* about this."

I don't answer. I just hide a smile and start walking, fast, in the general direction of the ocean.

It's high noon.

The Clock just struck.

30

WHERE EXACTLY IS the boat we're looking for, Stanley?"

I don't answer right away. I know downhill will take us to the harbor, but . . . it's a really big area.

"We need the Maritime Museum. Which way is it?"

"We're far. It'll take a long time to walk there." Liberty eyes me carefully. "We should take a bus."

I stop, close my eyes, clench my fists. "No bus," I whisper.

"Bus." She grabs my arm and drags me forward. "How is it even any different from the school bus, Stanley? You can do this!"

But it *is* different. I always know where the school bus is taking me. But a public bus is full of unknowns. Strange crowds. Strange locations. You could get trapped going in the wrong direction. There's noise. Germs.

Still. She's right. We need to save some time—and save our legs. So I just nod slowly. We run downhill to a bus stop, and Liberty shoves me up the steps into the Metro bus, which is idling in a cloud of stinky diesel.

When the doors close, I feel like I've been swallowed into the guts of some zombie prison. "Are you sure this is the right bus?" I whisper to her. She nods.

What if we miss our stop? What if we can never get off? What if it takes us farther and farther away from where we need to be? What if some stranger bothers us, and there's no way to get away?

Liberty's oblivious to my internal freak-out. We each show our Trivia Quest badges to the driver, who lets us pass. Then she yanks me down into a seat and looks around like she owns the place. She settles in and pulls out her phone to text her mom yet again. I look over her shoulder—the same three words: *Not dead yet.*

"Don't make contact with the dirty surfaces," I whisper. "Don't touch that grimy metal pole with your hand then touch your phone. You'll transfer germs! Probably thousands of other people have put their hands right there!"

A few passengers are staring at us. An old Mexican lady across the aisle smiles at me. I try to smile back but I really just want to shrink into the floor and disappear.

What would John Lockdown do? How would he

handle this? He would lift the bus on his shoulders and fly us in a flash to our destination. He would wave his magic around, like Mr. Clean, and instantly disinfect the whole bus so it was new and perfect. He would turn it into our private vehicle, no other people staring at us. . . .

Aqua. Ochre. Aqua. Ochre. I close my eyes, and try to imagine John Lockdown performing epic bus disinfection.

But: diesel stink, perfume, stale cigarettes. The gross minty aroma of other people's gum. Body odor, grease. Someone's fast food. The filthy floor. People pressing in . . .

"Get a grip, Stanley," Liberty whispers. "Let's talk about the clue. Focus on Natasha. Who is she? And what is her other name?"

Okay, okay. I pull the small gold envelope out of my pocket.

> *There's a certain black boat*
> *and a superhero dame*
> *Called one and the same—*
> *Natasha's other name.*
> *That's where you need to go.*
> *You'll find it down below.*

"It's got to be Natasha Romanova, Liberty. And her

other name is the Black Widow. You've heard of the Black Widow, right? From the Avengers, and Iron Man, and—well, actually, she's from comics starting like in the 1960s. She was supposedly born into Russian royalty but then she was handed off as a newborn to a soldier dude who trained her for the KGB. That's after she trained as a ballerina—"

Liberty interrupts me. "That's all really interesting, Stan, but what's it got to do with the boat? Do we need to look for a boat named the *Black Widow*? Because that's *Natasha's other name*?"

"Yes. But we're not looking for just any old regular boat," I say. The bus sways onto Harbor Drive and without thinking, I grab the grimy metal pole. Ick.

Liberty nudges me. "Then what is it?"

I sigh with relief. It's almost time to get off.

"You'll see," I say.

31

WHEN MY DAD was really young, like, right out of high school, he joined the navy. He thought it would be a good way to be of service to his new country, and to learn, get some training.

He was stationed on a nuclear sub. He doesn't talk about it too often— I don't think he liked it all that much.

But one weekend, after Cal and I had been bugging him, asking a lot of questions about what being on a sub was like, he drove us downtown to visit the Maritime Museum. They have a Soviet sub from the 1970s there. It's not like the one my dad was on—it's ancient, a piece of history. But still, going down there and visiting that sub was pretty cool.

My dad said there was a nickname for those old

Foxtrot B-class Soviet subs—he thought they were called *Black Widows.*

"You're a trivia master, Stanley!" says Liberty as we walk up to the roped-off museum entry dock.

At the ticket window, a pale, skinny woman with red hair, bright red lipstick, and extremely blue eyes is sitting behind the desk. Something about her seems familiar.

Liberty elbows me. "That's got to be Natasha!"

I freeze in my tracks. "Wait," I murmur. "I think I know her . . . but I'm not sure . . ."

Liberty rolls her eyes at me and sighs. Then she steps up.

"Excuse me, ma'am. Um, are you supposed to be the Black Widow? I mean, Natasha?"

"Could be. Who wants to know?" The lady stares at us, eyes wide, and loudly pops a chewing gum bubble.

I know who she is now. I've just never seen her without her sunglasses.

"Black Widow," Liberty repeats. "As in, 'Natasha's other name? Did we get the clue?'"

I step forward. "Wait—are you—Olga? Is that you?"

My bus driver breaks into a grin. "Aha! Stanley! The keed from Canyon Rim, with the loud big brother." She gives me a thumbs up. "But I am not Olga today. I am as you have guessed: Natasha. My boyfriend, he is organizer. I go to Comic Fest every year as Black Widow. It's fun!" Then she slides two slips of paper under the glass. "Good guessing job, keeds! Here are your entry tickets!"

"Thanks, but aren't you supposed to give us a golden coin? And the next clue?" Liberty asks. But Olga—I mean Natasha—only winks and opens the gate. "Tickets good for submarine only," she says in her thick accent.

"I can't believe you know her!" whispers Liberty as we walk down the dock to the boats. Which makes me feel weirdly proud, although I'm not sure what exactly of.

We walk past several ships on display. There's the old-fashioned *Star of India*, with its tall masts and furled sails, and a little tugboat with rubber-tire bumpers all around it, to keep it from crunching into the dock. And finally, there it is, just as I remember: that *Black Widow* sub. Half submerged in the water, with a gangplank leading to its big black metal hull. A piece of history. A Soviet relic.

A museum attendant—or maybe it's just some old guy in a yachting cap—smiles and waves us up the gangplank.

We make our way to the open hatch, and I start down some steep metal steps. It quickly becomes dark and enclosed. The smell of machine oil and fuel reminds me of the bus.

At the bottom of the stairs, if I remember right, is the torpedo room. "Liberty?" I peer back up to where she's still hesitating on the top step. "Come on down!" The sunny sky behind her head makes me squint.

"What if I just wait for you up here?" she says in a wavering voice.

"Seriously? After all this, you're telling me *you're* afraid? Of the sub?" I climb halfway back up, and find her backing away from the hatch.

"It's too . . . small down there. Too closed in."

"You made me get on the bus. So now you can do this," I say firmly.

We stare each other down, until she finally sighs and inches toward the stairs.

I guess we all have different things that set us off.

The large, red-and-white painted torpedoes are the first things you notice as you step into the hold. I put my hand on their cold, hard surface. It doesn't *feel* dangerous. "Imagine you're deep underwater for months at a time, ready to kill or be killed at any moment," I say to her, going for high drama.

"Shut up." Liberty is breathing funny but she is inching forward with me, now, through the series of hatches.

"It's okay," I tell her. "You can do this. You're perfectly safe."

"So you're just loving this, right?" she snarls.

When we get to the kitchen, or mess, or whatever you call it on a submarine, we're surprised by two sailors, sitting still as statues at a tiny table. For a quick moment, I think they're dummies, part of the exhibit. They're wearing navy jackets with brass nametags: Anton Vanko, and Ivan Petrovitch.

Liberty hits her head on the low ceiling of the sub, she's so surprised to see them. "Ouch! Wait! They're real!"

I try not to laugh.

Their names sound like they are from the Black Widow comics, but I can't quite place them.

Anton Vanko, the Russian sailor on the left, lifts his eyebrows, waiting for us to approach.

"So, we're doing the Trivia Quest," Liberty says as I fish the clue envelope out of my pocket. "And Natasha at the ticket window, she's the Black Widow, right? Just like the sub. So . . . did we get it?"

Ivan Petrovitch smiles at her. "Wery good! You have half of it down. But here is part two of the clue: Which of us is the Black Widow's friend . . ."

" . . . And," Anton Vanko adds, "which of us is her foe?"

Which is friend and which is foe?

Liberty throws up her hands. "Don't look at me. "This is totally your wheelhouse, Stanley." She waits. "Speak,

Stanley!" She turns to the two men. "He's doesn't talk much, but he knows his stuff."

The two men stare at me expectantly. I fixate on their nametags. Friend and foe . . .

"Can he ask you hints?" suggests Liberty. "Like twenty questions?"

"Nyet," says Ivan Petrovitch, a steely blue glint in his eye.

"I bet Natasha back at the entrance would let us ask. She's Stanley's bus driver, you know. And she seems way nicer than you guys," Liberty says, stalling for time.

"Nyet," Ivan says. "My Natasha doesn't play games."

Suddenly, it clicks. "*Your* Natasha? Okay, Ivan Petrovitch. Then you must be the Russian soldier who rescued baby Natasha Romanova after her mother died in a fire, and raised her like your own. Your Natasha. Raised her to be a KGB agent. That was you, right? So that means you, Anton Vanko, must be the foe." I grin. I've got this! "Later," I add, "when she came to the Avengers, which is the series where most people start to know about her, you—"

Ivan Petrovitch raises his hand to cut me off, just when I get warmed up! Oh well. Then Anton Vanko reaches into a briefcase on the bench and hands Liberty a golden token—our third! And a new clue envelope!

We did it!

Liberty doesn't even say thanks, or *spasibo*, or whatever. She launches herself back through that submarine so fast she's like a human torpedo. I salute the two men, then follow her.

On the surface, the fresh ocean air smells so good. So much better than that dark, cramped space below us. Liberty clutches at my arm.

"I think—I know—a little better—how you feel sometimes, Stanley," she says, wheezing slightly.

I pat her on the back. "Name your favorite color, Liberty," I say. I'll teach you a little breathing trick."

32

I WONDER HOW Joon and Dylan are doing," I say as we head down the dock toward the exit.

"Don't worry about them. Just think—we have three gold tokens!" Liberty says. "Almost halfway there!"

"Yeah, but it's well past one o'clock," I say as we turn onto the harbor walkway. "Like three and a half hours left. And we need to get four more tokens. Plus—are you hungry?" My stomach gurgles.

"Starved," she says. "But first let's open the clue envelope."

We tear it open, and we both snort when we read it. Because it's like the clue heard my stomach growl or something.

"It's the best lunch spot," sez . . .
Lorena Marquez.

"That's it? Two measly lines?" Liberty says, her eyes wide. "From that long, complicated Black Widow clue, to this tiny short one?"

We walk back along the harbor promenade, thinking.

"I am pretty sure Lorena Marquez was one of the Aquagirls," I finally say. "I'm not a hundred percent sure. There've been a lot of Aquagirls."

Liberty exhales hard. "I don't get why they call the male superheroes men, like Superman, Batman, Aquaman. But the female superheroes are all called girls. Batgirl, Supergirl, Aquagirl."

"Well, there's Wonder Woman. And I think Lorena Marquez is supposed to be young, like in high school or something, so technically she *is* kind of a girl."

"If that's true," Liberty says, "then Peter Parker should be called Spider-*Boy* because he's supposed to be in high school, too. Sorry. It's not right."

"Agreed." I think about the busty, crazy-shaped women they have in a lot of those old issues. "A lot of stuff in the history of comics hasn't been fair to girls."

"A lot of stuff in *history* hasn't been fair to girls,"

Liberty says, jabbing me in the arm with her bony elbow. "But let's get back to the clue."

I look at the ocean, sparkling right out there, beyond the harbor's cluster of boats and ships. I imagine Aquaman and Aquagirl somewhere out there, swimming in their magical undersea world—looking for . . .

. . . the best lunch spot? Seriously. Weird clue.

"Let's go find food," says Liberty, turning inland toward the city and a nearby park. "Are you at least *somewhat* sure Lorena Marquez is Aquagirl?"

"Yeah." I glance back at the ocean. "In fact I think she was the Aquagirl in this cool series Joon has, called *Sub Diego*."

"Tell me about it."

"Okay . . . Imagine a typical sunny San Diego day like today. Lorena Marquez is a teenager, hanging with a friend at the zoo. Suddenly, there's this level-one-million-on-the-Richter-scale earthquake, and half of San Diego drops into the ocean."

Liberty's eyes bulge.

I stare at the calm, still water beyond us, and think back to when Principal Coffin had a tsunami drill. We had to get on school buses and drive really fast uphill and inland, as if we were trying to outrace the rising monster tides.

I shudder. I didn't like this Aquaman/Aquagirl

story line. Joon laughed at me, but I didn't want to read about my own town getting wiped off the map. Could it happen? It's happened to other places in the world. It's happened to people my dad has helped get back on their feet.

Liberty nudges me. "Go on. Does everybody die?"

"No. They don't die. They morph—they grow gills, and end up creating a whole underwater city called Sub Diego, submerged off the coast."

"Gills," says Liberty, whistling. "So they adapt and evolve, happily ever after?"

"Not exactly. The gills are because—unbeknownst to them—the people of Sub Diego have been genetically manipulated for evil corporate aims of world domination—you know, the usual drill. Aquaman and Aquagirl try to fix everything."

"Cool," Liberty says, getting out her phone to text her mom again. "A submerged city."

"Yeah," I say. "*Sub Diego.*"

Click.

I look down at the small card in my hand while Liberty texts *not dead yet* to her mom again.

Click.

Lorena Marquez's favorite lunch spot . . .

"Remember when we were studying in my room and talking about all the food trucks around here?"

"Yeah. Phil's BBQ, the sushi truck."

"Yeah. And the sub sandwich truck. Sub Diego."

Our stomachs growl at the same time. We both smile.

33

WATERFRONT PARK IS a big long stretch of public green space, benches, fountains, playgrounds, and walking paths. But all Liberty and I care about are the food trucks parked around its borders.

Or, to be more precise: one particular food truck.

"Let's split up," says Liberty. You take that side, I'll take this one. First one who finds the Sub Diego sandwich truck, texts the other."

Meanwhile, people are pouring into the park from everywhere, in groups, laughing, talking. A police siren wails. I hate that noise. It makes the pulse of a headache start up behind my right eye. "Shouldn't we just stay together?" I say. "It's getting crowded."

"It's downtown! What do you expect?" Liberty pats

me on the head. I hate being patted on the head. "Just text me if you find it." Then she slips out of sight behind a big group of people carrying coolers and lawn chairs. She's gone, like she fell into a crack in the earth or something. Just like in Sub Diego.

Okay, okay. I need to stop worrying, and start scouting food trucks. But first, I think I need to find a bathroom.

I wander around until I spy a row of bright blue plastic port-a-johns at the far end of the park, just past a big outdoor stage. Security guys in headphones are strolling around near it. Guys in black T-shirts are testing speakers and checking cables. And I realize that this is where all the people are heading. It's filling up by the minute! I guess there's going to be some kind of concert or show.

I hurry past, almost tripping on a bright yellow power cord.

When I've found the least disgusting port-a-john in the row, and I'm finally relieving myself:

BLAM!

It sounds like a speaker just exploded. The whole port-a-john vibrates. I jump two feet in the air. And, as I jump, the unthinkable happens . . . My cell phone tumbles out of my shorts pocket and into the open hole.

Noooo!

I grab for it in horror-movie slow motion, but it's no

use. The phone's already sliding down, down into oblivion.

I let out a small shriek as the loudspeaker blares again. Do they have it mounted on the top of this port-a-john or something? The walls shake. *"Gather 'round, partiers! Our Saturday lunchtime concert series kicks off at one-thirty on the south stage with verrrry special guests!"*

I stumble out of there, gulping fresh air. There is now a line waiting in front of the row of port-a-johns. I feel dazed and confused. I tell the next person—a stocky dude in mirror sunglasses and a Mickey Mouse shirt—"My phone! It fell into the, uh, the . . ."

He steps backward away from me.

"I need my phone!" I cry out.

"And I need to pee before Blue Paloma starts playing," the guy says.

I veer away, trying to remember where I left Liberty. But now the crowd's grown into a giant mob. I get swept up in a wave of people and carried off into a roped area by the stage where we all just stand still. Nowhere to go.

"Excuse me," I shout. "Let me through, please!" But no one moves. It's like I'm invisible. Red Alerts are wooping through my chest.

"Excuse me!" I say, louder now, and a lady budges about six inches to the right. I squeeze through—only to face a mass of more people. In fact, this whole roped-in

169

area around the stage has somehow magically turned into a solid block of wall-to-wall humanity. We're packed tight as sardines in a can, and everyone's buzzing and talking and pushing and shoving me around in their quest for the best spot to see Blue Paloma.

Blue Paloma. The "verrry special guests." The group that plays on Olga's bus radio. Boy, what Gaby Garcia and the seventh-grade girls would give to see this.

But me? I need to get out of here.

More people arrive every second, flowing in impossible waves. I push against the tide like a salmon struggling upstream. Strangers' arms and legs press into me as I get bumped and tossed.

Red Alert!

Red Alert!

My heart feels like a scared rabbit thumping inside my chest. I make a strange bleating cry, and a few bewildered faces flash in my direction, then turn away.

If I fall, I'll get trampled.

Maybe I'm having a heart attack.

It's like when I was five, and I lost Dad once, in a crowd at a rally. The same panic has my chest in an iron grip.

The drums from Blue Paloma jump-start the beat.

One—Two—Three—Four—

My heart is exploding in my chest. I'm choking,

drowning! I need my dad! My mom! Somebody! Liberty!

I need John Lockdown! What would John Lockdown do?

I close my eyes and imagine him flying overhead. Yelling at the crowd to part in his booming voice.

I need to yell at the crowd to part.

Suddenly I'm sucking in air, then shouting: "LET ME THROUGH!" I yell at the top of my lungs, tears streaming down my face. **"LET ME THROUGH!"**

Next to me a sweaty man in a Blue Paloma shirt finally notices me. "Hey, kid," he shouts over the noise, looking confused. "Don't you want to see the concert?" I shake my head and point toward the exit. He turns sideways and lets me squeeze past.

"Hey!" he calls out to the next person in the crowd. "Let this kid through, will you? He doesn't look too good!"

And then, as if by some miracle, the chant goes along the line, like a telephone chain, one person calling after the other. "Hey, let this kid through! He's sick! Hey! Let him pass!"

It's weird. The crowd is my worst nightmare, but instead of getting devoured and un-existed by them—the crowd helps me.

"Kid coming through!" people keep calling out.

A scary biker dude with piercings and tattoos puts his

hands under my armpits and lifts me high up in the air, which is terrifying—until he pivots me around, points me past him, and puts me gently back on the ground even closer to the exit. I'm too stunned to even react.

But I keep moving.

After what seems like ten eons of struggling past arms and legs and bellies and sweaty bodies, my heart pounding, blood rushing in my ears, my throat parched and tight—I sense I'm nearly out. An old hippie lady with long, curly gray hair turns to me with a kind smile. "Here you go, honey," she says, lifting up the final rope barrier.

And I'm out. I'm home free.

I run away from the concert pavilion toward the open green space, sweating and panting and having Red Alerts like crazy. Finally, I throw myself down under a tree and curl into a small ball.

BOOM. BOOM. BOOM.

I cover my ears but the whiny guitar strains and drumbeats of Blue Paloma still waft around me. The crowd back there is still roaring, but at least it's a dull roar now. "Hold on," the song goes. "Hold on, baby, hold on."

I've heard it before on the school bus. *Hold on.*

You know what? I really, really hate Blue Paloma.

34

SINCE MY PHONE got port-a-johnned, I can't call Liberty. Who knows where she went? I slump down on a bench near where we split up.

I'm done. I want to go home. I close my eyes and pretend if I shut out the world, it will leave me alone.

But the sun's too strong, a pulsing red under my eyelids. The voices of people buzzing around me are too nerve-racking. With a sigh, I sit back up.

Mom is probably going to kill me for losing that phone. Now I don't even know what time it is. Must be well after two. And Liberty and I will probably never finish the Trivia Quest. I'm nothing but a big loser, yet again. I've lost Liberty. I'll lose the contest. I've lost Joon as my best friend. Lost my dad. Lost my phone. My stomach tightens. My fists clench. I want to scream, but it's myself I'm angry at.

I don't know how much time goes by like that, with me on the bench, eyes shut, hands over my ears, before I sense a shadow falling across my face.

I open my eyes.

It's Bustamante. He slides onto the bench and nudges me in the side. "Dude," he says. "What up?"

I sit up straighter, feeling both glad and bummed to see him.

Then, out of the crowd, there's Joon. He sits down on the other side of me and nods, like nothing's unusual. He picks at a hangnail.

"Blue Paloma's playing," Joon says.

I nod.

"Why are you in the park? Is there a clue in the park? How many clues have you solved?" says Dylan.

"Where's Liberty?" Joon asks.

"I don't know. I lost her," I say. "AND my phone." I hold out my empty hands. "It hasn't been that great a day so far."

"I hear you," Dylan says, nodding. "This Quest thing is miserable, isn't it? Who could figure this stuff out? It's nuts! We solved the first clue. Since then, we've been stumped."

"Yeah," adds Dylan. "Since then we've just been

hanging out. Checking out the shops, walking around the boardwalk. This park's pretty cool."

"You solved *one* clue?" I whisper.

"Yeah. At Petco Park," Joon says. "A baseball clue about Batman. Get it? *Bat* man. A ticket taker named Robin gave us the gold coin." He digs in his pocket and holds it up sadly, watching it reflect the light. "Our only coin."

"You shouldn't tell me the clue," I say quickly, frowning. "We're not supposed to share information. What if I get that one later on?"

Joon rolls his eyes. Dylan says, "Later on? So—you're still in the running? How many clues have *you* solved?"

"We're working on the fourth."

Joon and Dylan look at each other. Dylan whistles. "Seriously?" Joon says. "Show us the coins."

"I can't. Liberty has them."

"Yeahhhh," says Dylan. "Riiiight." He winks knowingly.

"No, really," I say. "She does. But I lost her."

Joon shakes his head and sighs.

And that's when I get mad. "You act like I'm such a screwup. But I'm not! Look!" I pull the small gold envelopes out of my pocket and fan them out like playing cards.

When Joon and Dylan see the envelopes, they sit up a

little straighter. Which makes me feel a little better.

"And don't worry about Liberty," I say. "She'll be right back. We have the rest of the Quest to finish!"

Joon studies my face for a minute. Then he shrugs. "Okay, Stan. Whatever." He stands and dusts off his hands.

"Yeah!" adds Dylan. "We're going over to the concert. Good luck!" They head off into the crowd.

"Don't try to pretend you don't care about this, Joon!" I call after them. "Go ahead and listen to your dumb music! I'm gonna win Comic Fest tickets without you, do you hear? I'm gonna finish the Trivia Quest, Joon! With Liberty! I'm winning it! Do you hear me?"

He must hear. But he doesn't turn around.

Blue Paloma's been playing for a while—it's got to be around 2:00 p.m. Four more clues to get through in three hours or so? Is that even possible? But without Liberty, it's all over. If we don't find each other, I might as well just go back down to the convention center and just wait for the Quest to end and for Mrs. Lee to pick us up.

Just as I'm starting to seriously consider that, I notice her head bobbing above the crowd.

"Liberty!" I stand up, shout, and wave—then collapse back on the bench, limp with relief.

She's got two take-out bags with the bright blue

logo of Sub Diego. "Lunch!" Liberty says, waving them. "And I got the clue! I told them what you told me about Aquaman and Lorena Marquez. And the lady at the grill gave me sandwiches for free! And this!" She digs in her pocket and shows me the newest gold token. "I texted you like a million times—where the heck were you?"

"Lost my phone. Long story."

I think about trying to explain about the port-a-john, the lost phone, and my Blue Paloma panic attack. About bumping into Joon and Dylan, who aren't even competing anymore. How a few minutes ago, I was ready to quit, too.

But not now.

"Liberty, you're . . . ," I say then suddenly get tongue-tied. I want to tell her she's great, for helping me through. We don't even know each other that well, but here she is, going through this whole ordeal with me.

She hands me a sandwich. I manage to squeak: "Thanks."

She smiles. I figure she knows I don't just mean for the lunch.

35

INSIDE THE NEW envelope there is a hard lump that feels like a stubby crayon or something. When we tear the paper and peek in, we see a small carrot. Along with our next clue card.

> *Find the Captain of the Crew*
> *Just'a lotta fun for you!*

"How can a clue seriously be only two lines? Do they expect us to be mind readers? Are we supposed to have some kind of comic-strip clue-solving superpowers? I mean, you do, I guess. But I don't. What the heck?" Liberty grumbles, licking mayonnaise off her hand.

"*Captain of the Crew*? Maybe that's another boat

reference. Something by the harbor."

"Okay. Who else is a captain?" she asks. "In comic trivia, I mean."

"There's a bunch. For starters, there's the new Captain Marvel. But she doesn't have a crew, unless you could call the Starjammers a crew," I say, crumpling up my sandwich wrapper. "Then there's Captain America. He was part of the Avengers, but I'm not sure I'd call the Avengers his crew, if you know what I mean. Iron Man sure wouldn't!"

"So what superhero leads a crew?"

A memory is bumping around in my head. At Joon's about a month ago, he was waving around one of those silly Captain Carrot and the Zoo Crew comics. It's a Justice League of America spoof, with a tagline reading *Just'a Lotta Animals!*

I read the clue card again: *Just'a lotta fun for you . . .*

I wiggle the orange carrot from the envelope between my thumb and forefinger, and I know I've got it! I explain as Liberty crumples up her lunch bag.

"Well, it's pretty clear where we've got to go," she says. "But are you up to it? It means another bus ride. And you sure look pale."

I don't exactly *want* to but I've got to keep going. I need to prove something. To Joon. And Dylan. To . . . Keefner. To Principal Coffin, Mrs. Ngozo, Mom. To Dad.

And Gramps, and Calvin. To Liberty.

To John Lockdown.

And to myself.

But mainly to Joon.

So I nod.

"You know what my uncle used to tell me last year, when I felt really sick?" Liberty says. "He'd say: 'To get through hell, keep going.'"

I want to ask her that. About being sick. But now's not the time. She's already grabbing my arm and pulling me up off the bench, shouting: "To the zoo!"

36

THE SAN DIEGO Zoo is huge. And it's only one part of Balboa Park, a sprawling, monster campus of museums and parks and such. And it's far away enough from Waterfront Park to mean taking another stupid bus.

Argh!

I squirm in my sticky plastic seat. Liberty turns and stares down the lady across from me, who's shooting us dirty looks. "Stop staring at him," she snaps. "Haven't you seen car sickness before?"

"That's the trouble, kid," the lady says, glancing at me nervously. "I *have*."

It's 2:35 p.m. when the bus coughs us out at the zoo parking lot. Time's a wasting. Because we don't know what else to do, or where else to go, we join the hordes at

181

the tickets-and-information window.

The people behind us keep knocking the back of my knees with their huge stroller full of drooling toddlers, and the family ahead has a drooling toddler, too—it keeps staring at us over its father's shoulder. The line is taking forever. I'm about to explode with impatience when suddenly, a burst of music blares over the speakers, and a bunch of costumed mascots come out to entertain the crowd.

A striped tiger holds a sign for the Tiger Trail. A couple of black-and-white pandas show a banner for the panda exhibit. And then this mangy, skinny, orange bunny with ridiculous floppy ears strolls out a side gate. He's not holding any sign—he just stands there, scanning the crowd with his hands on his hips.

I look at Liberty. She looks at me.

"That's got to be him—Captain Carrot!" she says. "Go on! Go over to him, Stanley!"

I squirm. "That's your job!"

Liberty puts her hands on her hips. "No way. I've done most of the talking all day."

"So what?" I say, feeling nervous. "I solve the clues, and you do the talking. That's our deal."

Liberty scowls at me but she goes over to the rabbit. He has no idea that she's behind him so when she taps his shoulder, he jumps a foot in the air. I laugh as I watch her flutter her hands around, talking fast. He stands perfectly still, listening to her explain the Zoo Crew clue. Then the rabbit puts a small piece of paper and a golden coin into Liberty's hand. She jumps up and down and does a little dance.

Then, the rabbit starts jumping with her. Suddenly they are doing the strangest dance moves I've ever seen. Fist-pumping, hip-bumping, roof-raising—and is that mangy rabbit actually trying to beatbox?

Now here comes Liberty, waving her arms at me. "Bust a move, Stanley," she shouts, grabbing my hand. "You don't have to talk. Just dance!" She and the rabbit pull me in and won't let go. Captain Carrot is a terrible beatboxer—he can barely keep a rhythm—but I bob my head around a little, feeling like an idiot. All the people in line are staring at us.

I try to do the robot. I am awful at it. But the drooling toddlers in line are mesmerized—and they start dancing, too! Then their parents start in, and before you know it, the mangy rabbit is prancing around them, and the whole line is bopping.

I grab Liberty's hand. If there ever was a time to sneak away from Captain Carrot and the world's worst dance party, it's now.

37

CAPTAIN RABBIT SAID we're only the tenth team that's gotten the Zoo Crew clue—out of the hundreds of people at the plaza this morning. Seriously! Can you believe that?"

"His name is Captain Carrot," I tell Liberty, as we stroll into the zoo, our fifth golden coin tucked safely into her pack. "And that's great, but let's not get too excited. There are lots of possible clues," I say. "It could be that only a small group of us got this one."

"Or, it could be that we're awesome at this, and we're going to win those VIP passes!" She gives my shoulder a punch. "Don't you think? I'm sure of it!"

I'm not sure of anything. It's already 3:30. We have about ninety minutes to solve this clue and the next one, and then get back down to the plaza before the Quest ends.

And the message on the little card in my hand is pretty cryptic.

> *It's to be found*
> *Where Vertebrate DCs*
> *Are flipped around.*

"Vertebrate DCs, flipped around? That's gibberish," I say. "What are DCs? Data Collection Systems? Digital Computer Systems?"

"Duck Call Sounds?" Liberty says as we walk past a quacking pond full of them.

I sigh.

"But it's DCs flipped around," Liberty says. "So does that mean CDs? Like compact discs? Are we looking for old-fashioned music?"

I snort. "Don't forget the word 'Vertebrate.' Maybe both words get flipped, or written backward. Let's see. That makes—CD Etarbetrev. Maybe that means something in Latin? Russian?"

Now it's her turn to snort. "Well, what's 'flipped around' mean? That's the key. When something's flipped around, it's backward, or inside out, or opposite."

185

A thought hits me. "Well, backward doesn't seem to work. So what about opposites?"

"Well," she says as we cruise past the panda exhibit, "what does vertebrate mean? Having a spine, right? So the opposite is *in*vertebrate."

"And what about DCs? What's the opposite of that?" Another flash of an idea hits me. "Maybe we're supposed to sound it out. DCs. That sounds like . . . Decease. Or disease. A spine disease? Are we looking for a place where there's a spine disease? Maybe some animal at the zoo has a spinal problem?"

Liberty frowns. "But that doesn't explain 'flipped around.' The opposite of vertebrate is invertebrate—spineless. That's something, I guess. But what about DCs?"

I have another thought. "Liberty, we're forgetting this is Trivia Quest. The answer has to have something to do with comics."

"Yeah, so—?"

"So—DC. As in DC Comics. What's the opposite, or the opposing comic company, to DC Comics?"

She just looks at me.

"Gah! It's Marvel, right? DC's rival comic company. So if we flip DC around to its opposite, we get Marvel. . . ."

I'm getting a headache. It's hard to breathe. The

minutes are ticking by.

Liberty runs off to grab a zoo map, and we sit down on a bench to study it. "Let's just see what's on here that has to do with invertebrates, or with comics companies," she says.

I gasp. I see it before she does. A small dot, over by the reptile house, representing an insect exhibit.

According to the map key, the name of the exhibit is *Spineless Marvels*.

Vertebrate DCs, flipped around. Totally.

38

LIBERTY'S BEEN TEXTING her mom constantly, all day. But for the first time, as we're speed-walking to Spineless Marvels, her phone starts beeping with texts back.

"What's going on?" I ask.

"My mom. Something . . . weird." She shakes her head, as if to shake off the thought. "She's such a worrier!" Liberty shoves her phone in her jeans pocket. "I'm putting it away. Okay. Sorry."

We jog down the path—we have to hurry—but before I know it, she's stopped again, texting.

"What's it about?"

She presses her lips into a tight line. "Nothing."

We jog-walk a bit further. Liberty's abnormally silent.

"I've just been thinking: Why are cowards called

spineless?" I ask, just for something to say. At this point, we're almost through the children's zoo, past clumps of kids petting goats. "And why do they say brave people have backbones?"

"I dunno. I think sometimes being brave is being flexible," she says. "Think of how an octopus changes its shape. I'm not talking Spider-Man's Dr. Octopus. Just regular octopi. I read about an octopus in Australia that contorted itself all the way down something like a half mile of drainpipe to escape out to the sea."

"Wow."

"Yeah. So spineless can be brave. There are definitely different kinds of strength," she says. She exhales hard. "For instance, dealing with my mom? That definitely takes a kind of flexible strength. And . . . I hope you can be flexible, too, Stan." Her eyes are a darker, cloudier green than usual.

I frown. I want to ask what she means, but we're already standing in front of the insect exhibit. "Well," Liberty says, "we're not here for octopus, Stanley. We're here for bugs. Creepy crawlies. Spineless Marvels."

Inside, in the dim light, all kinds of hairy-legged monsters scurry and lurk in their tanks. I don't want to get too close. But Liberty coos at them like they're kittens. She pulls me over to these little brown ants carrying green leaf parts above their heads like sails.

Apparently they chew and spit out leaf gunk into holes underground, to ferment, like spitty leaf-beer.

Ugh.

"Just open your eyes and look at them! Honestly. They are adorable!" she says, yanking me over to the tank. "And look at this one!"

The sign says *Jungle Nymph*. It's a bright green leaf eater from Malaysia, almost the length of my forearm. Apparently, it tries to impale enemies with its legs.

Nice.

"Liberty," I whisper. "What time is it?"

"It's 3:45."

My stomach lurches. "Let's find the golden token and get the heck out of here!"

"Okay! But would you look at this?" She points to a tank where a brown-shelled monster with a huge head, beady eyes, and tiny teeth rambles around like it's on fully charged batteries. "Dragon headed katydid. Scariest-looking bug ever—but in reality, completely harmless and friendly." She nudges me, with a shy look on her face. "See? Things can look scary at first, but turn out just fine. Just like today. Right, Stan?"

"Today's not over yet," I mutter.

Next to the horrific yet harmless katydid is a New Guinea stick insect. It's got a big long exoskeleton with barbs or points on it. The sign says they can snap their legs together, or curl their ovipositors—egg-laying parts—and even fling eggs at attackers.

"The ovipositors are overheating, Captain!" Liberty says, waving her arms around. "Eject the dilithium crystals!"

I can't even laugh. This race against time is starting to get to me. I'm ready to lose it, when the back door to the exhibit finally opens and a man in thick glasses and a white lab coat comes in. On his lapel is a name tag that reads *Dr. Pym*.

Now we're talking!

"See his lab coat?" I whisper to Liberty. "You know who Hank Pym was, right? Every hear of Pym Particles? They shrink matter down to microscopic and even submicroscopic size. This guy is the creator of Ant-Man!"

I say the name "Ant-Man" kind of louder than I mean to, and Dr. Pym glances over.

That clinches it.

"Go ask him, Liberty!" I whisper.

"No way," she says, folding her arms. "I'm not covering for you anymore. Speak up for yourself."

I try puppy-dog eyes and a little bit of whimpering, but she just folds her arms harder. And the time is ticking.

So I take a deep breath, and walk up to the man in the lab coat.

"Excuse me, sir. Invertebrates are spineless, and DC's

rival is Marvel, and we're on the Trivia Quest. And it's an honor to meet the creator of Ant-Man." I wipe my sweaty palms on my jeans and hold out my hand. My heart is thumping, but it's thumped so much today, I figure I might as well ignore it.

He shakes my hand, gives a little bow, and says, "Excellent work! You have it exactly right, indeed, young man. Why, in fact, Ant-Man is inside that exhibit right now, transmitting important information about the Comic Fest to his leaf-cutter allies."

He says this so seriously, it's almost like he believes it. Then Dr. Pym fishes in the deep pockets of his white lab coat, and pulls out a golden token and a small envelope.

"Well done, young entomologists," he whispers. "You've done it! Best be on your way." He looks at his watch. "It's almost four o'clock. The time you've got left is, shall we say, *shrinking dramatically*."

39

WE'VE GOT ONLY one measly hour left to solve our final clue, and then get back down to the finish at the convention plaza. And the travel time alone could take up a half hour. I feel Red Alerts starting to hit me, as I race back through the zoo behind Liberty on our way to the exit.

It's going to be tight. We might not make it. And that thought leaves me more breathless than the running.

When we're by the bus and shuttle area, I start to rip open our final envelope—but Liberty puts a hand on my arm to stop me.

"Stanley. Wait. I'm really sorry—I wanted to tell you this earlier." She seems nervous, and keeps looking out at the road. "But I figured I'd wait until you solved the

Pym clue so it wouldn't distract you."

"Liberty! We have to read this next clue *now*!"

"No! Hold on." Liberty tents her hands over her nose and mouth, like she's afraid to let the words she's about to say escape her mouth. Finally, she takes her hands away and exhales loudly. "Stanley, sorry to tell you this. But I have to go."

"What?"

What the heck did she just say?

"I have to go. Back when I was at the park, I felt kind of sick and light-headed, and I stupidly mentioned it to my mom in a text. It was just hunger. Or maybe all that coffee. But what do you know, big surprise, she freaked out. She never wanted me to be running around downtown. So now she's driving all the way down here—two hours, from LA."

"Driving down here?" I'm confused.

Liberty cringes and hunches up her shoulders. "To pick me up. She's almost here."

I just stare at her. Her words don't make sense. How can this be? Leave? What is she talking about?

"Hel-LO, Stan? You in there?" She waves her hands in front of my dazed eyes. "I can't compete with you anymore today. Get it? My mom's coming to get me. You have to finish the Quest alone."

"You're leaving?"

"Yeah. She's mad at my uncle; she's mad at me; she's convinced this running around was too much." She shakes her head. "I'm *fine*! She's *crazy* overprotective. I told you. Ever since--"

"--Ever since what? Why is she so overprotective?" I say. "You're the most independent person I know! Just text your mom back, tell her to wait at your Uncle Dan's. We're almost done!"

Liberty's mouth turns into a sad grimace. I think she's going to cry. "You don't know her. I can't change her mind. And besides," she says, pointing down the drive, "there she is!"

I feel this explosive ball of urgency, fear, and panic growing inside me. I want to shout at her. But she looks so sad and defeated.

We watch a dented old Jeep Wrangler pull up to the curb. A lady with long bushy red hair sticks her head out the window and yells, "Baby, get in this car right now!"

Liberty and I stare at each other without saying a word. "It's 4:00 p.m., Stan," she tells me. "Just one more hour. You can do it. Be flexible. Like the octopus. Brave and flexible."

"Liberty!" shouts her mom. "Make that boy come with us! Both of you get in the car!"

"I guess I can handle one hour," I say. But my voice is trembling.

"Good! I'm shooting you brain waves of superpower!" She widens her green eyes until they're bulging, and wiggles her fingers at me.

It's stupid, but it makes me smile.

Then she gets in the Jeep and shouts, "Bye, Stanley! I'm so sorry!" as it pulls out with a roar and a puff of black smoke.

And that's when I realize Liberty still has all our gold coins in her pocket.

40

FOR A SPLIT second, I stand there, frozen, as crowds of people brush past. Then, a bolt of electric energy shoots through me, and I sprint down the road, charging after that Jeep.

There's a nice big bright red traffic light up ahead. If I'm lucky, they're at it.

If I'm unlucky, they're gone.

I sprint up to the light, checking every car. Not them. Not them. Not them . . .

Them! In the left turn lane, two lanes up from where I'm standing. I have to cross over to the concrete island to get to them—then, I bang on the window hard enough to rattle the glass. Liberty's mother turns, swift and surprised, her mouth a giant O.

With a glance at the red light, she lowers the window, and I notice Liberty's face, over in the passenger seat, is stained with tears.

"Liberty! The coins!"

Liberty's mom swears under her breath. "Get out of this intersection before you get hit! I'll pull over. Just— cross the street over there," she orders me.

A moment later at the curb, Liberty quickly gets out. Her cheeks are dried and her face is flushed. "Sorry, Stanley," she says, quickly handing over the tokens and map.

Her mother peers at me over her sunglasses like I'm some sort of threatening strain of bacteria. "I shouldn't be leaving you here," she says. "I think you should get in the car. How old are you?"

"Mom!" shouts Liberty, offended. "Stan's small, but he's old enough. He can handle it. In fact, Stanley's one of the bravest kids I know."

I snort.

"Swear to God. Stanley's scared of everything, Mom. But he's sticking it out!" She gives me a thumbs up.

They pull away, with Mrs. Silverberg still shaking her head and muttering. Liberty sticks her hand out the window, and makes a power fist.

I'm pretty mad at her, but still, I raise my fist back, my fingers closed tightly around our six golden coins.

41

IT'S 4:20. JUST thinking about that fact makes my stomach lurch.

I'm alone in Balboa Park.

Where do I go from here?

What would John Lockdown do?

Maybe he'd start with first things first. Like: breathing. And zipping the coins into my pack.

And now, the final clue. The one from Dr. Pym.

I hold it up with shaking fingers and stare at it. All I see is panicked squiggles. I force my brain to turn them into actual letters and words. Words I need to read. A clue I need to solve. I will keep competing. I will win this thing. Not for Liberty. Not for Joon. Not for Mom. Not even for John Lockdown. But for me now. Just for me.

Faster than a locomotive,
this model citizen
saves his 'model' city.

Faster than a locomotive? This is an easy clue! That's
Superman. Bends steel with his bare hands, et cetera.
And Superman, just like John Lockdown, is a do-gooder,
the Good Guy, the ultimate *model* citizen. Right?

And *model city*. San Diego's motto is "America's Finest
City." Is a finest city the same thing as a model city?

I'm feeling the deafening silence of no one to talk to
about this.

Think. Think think think.

My dad would say there's no such a thing as a model
city. He'd say all cities, and all places, have problems.
Because all *people* have problems.

I remember him showing me a photo, before he left,
of a paper model his charity organization had made. It
was on a big board, a white model of a small village center with a new well and a school and a health clinic. . . .

Model city.

Okay. Now I have an idea.

I jog quickly around until I find a stop for the little
trolley shuttle, the one that goes around to the different
areas within Balboa Park, and when it comes, I board,

even though I'm shaking with nerves. I double-check with the driver: "Excuse me, do you know where the Model Railroad Museum is? Do you stop near it?"

He nods.

I hop on and quickly take a seat. I stare out the window to be sure I don't miss the stop.

A few minutes later, he pulls up by some arched, covered walkways. I step off, and take a deep breath. I don't see any signs for a Model Railroad Museum. Now I'm shaking again.

Woop.

Woop.

I jog down one side of the walkway, and up the other. Finally, just past a restaurant and a gift shop, I spy it!

The place is smaller than I remembered. Dad took Calvin and me here a really long time ago. I remember the action figures and Matchbox cars in the little street scenes set up around the train tracks.

I'm hoping against hope that one of those action figures is Superman.

I look at a wall clock. 4:15.

Woop.

Woop.

The place is filled with big tabletop displays—model cities—of tiny villages, mountains, and farms, through which rumbling model trains chug and puff. *Faster than a locomotive/this model citizen/saves his "model" city.* Where is he?

I run from one layout to the next, scanning the tiny main streets, side streets, farms, trains, bridges, forests, and tunnels. My heart's pounding as I race.

Where are you, Superman?

My gaze lands on a scene by a lake; there's a tiny fisherman with a fish on his line, the rod back behind his shoulder. A little plastic bear is coming out of the woods behind him, about to steal his fish.

And parked in front of the general store is a model of Scooby-Doo's mystery van. A chicken truck is overturned on the road, and a wolf—or is it a coyote?—is slinking away with one of the chickens.

But no Superman.

It's like a high-stress *Where's Waldo?* My eyes scan tiny schools, restaurants, gas stations, surf shops, candy stores, ice cream parlors, hardware stores, and farms with little fake cows and goats. There are roadways with vintage toy cars, painted plaster hills, and rough rocks beyond, and then taller mountains with a giant suspension bridge, way back against the wall, and then . . .

"I found him!" I shout. An old man in an engineer's cap and apron with a volunteer badge turns and looks at me. "Superman!" I explain. "Helping out his model city! Like in the Trivia Quest clue! Right?"

The little plastic Superman action figure is lying flat, his hands grasping the train rails on a broken section of bridge, his feet hooking the rails behind. He's completing the track with his body, so the train, when it comes, won't tumble down into the gorge. A classic Superman-to-the-rescue move. He's a model citizen saving his model city all right.

The old man in the engineer's cap smiles at me and presses a button. A sleek, orange and silver engine with a bright single headlight makes its way out of the tunnel and crosses, clickety-clack, over Superman's stretched-out body.

The train takes a bend, goes through another tunnel, then turns to descend into town. It slows to a gradual stop right in front of me.

Inside its empty coal car is a shiny golden token.

"Wow!" I turn to the engineer, smiling. "Thanks!"

He nods and checks his pocket watch. "How many clues did you find today?"

"This was my seventh one!"

His eyebrows shoot up. "Whoa!" he says. "You're a grand-prize VIP pass winner!" He glances at his watch again, and strokes his beard. "That is, you will be—if you can back get down to the plaza within . . . 24.5 minutes!"

I dash out the door.

42

BARBARA GORDON/BATGIRL. Brian O'Brien/the Clock. Natasha Romanov/the Black Widow. Lorena Marquez/ Aquagirl. Ridiculous dancing Captain Carrot. And Dr. Hank Pym, and Superman. That's seven.

What a day. I've port-a-johnned my phone, faced smothering crowds, and had a meltdown at Blue Paloma. I faced deafening noise, stinky buses, and my own fear. I've run all over town. I've lost my partner.

And I almost lost the tokens. Right now, they are zipped carefully into my backpack's side pocket. Seven tokens that belong to Liberty and me. Meanwhile, the big city Metro bus I'm riding in—please, John Lockdown, keep me safe—rumbles and bumps down the hill.

I unzip the pocket, reach in, and touch them, rubbing

204

my thumb across the raised letter *Q*, for *Quest*, on each smooth, round surface.

I can turn in these seven tokens for two VIP passes to Comic Fest. I let that sink in, maybe for the first time. *Two VIP passes to Comic Fest!*

I wonder how Liberty is doing. Her mom seemed like she was having a meltdown of her own. A worry-meltdown. But Liberty was fine. Why did her mom feel she had to take her away?

All kinds of troubles in the world, says John Lockdown.

I stare out the smudged bus window at the passing view. I'm in the first seat, all tensed up and ready to fly out the door, the instant we get to the convention center.

We pass under a bridge, where a homeless man with a shopping cart and pieces of cardboard is shuffling around. I think, again, of Rorschach in disguise.

At an intersection, business people brush past with briefcases, talking on their phones. A few skateboarders are on the sidewalk, laughing, shouting.

Through the front windshield is the ocean. The heavy orange ball of the sun hovers a few inches over the silver, calm water of the harbor. I breathe in.

I start rocking impatiently in my seat—like that's going to make the bus go faster. I know we should probably turn left, when we hit the harbor, because the conference center is south of the airport. But when we hit Harbor Drive, the bus swings neatly around to the right.

Do I say something? Maybe this is what's supposed to happen. Maybe we're making a U-turn or something.

We accelerate. I see signs for the airport.

Red Alert!

Red   Alert!

Fear opens my mouth. I find myself grasping the arm of the man next to me and asking: "Please—aren't we going to the convention center?"

He looks surprised. "No! You're on the bus to Mission Bay, kid."

Everything stops. Space. Time. Sound.

Is my heart even still beating?

"Kid, you okay?" The man shoots a worried glance up at the bus driver. "Hey!" I hear him shout. "This kid here looks like he's gonna faint!"

43

IN ORDER TO get the bus driver to let me off, I have to lie. I have to tell her my mom's waiting for me in her car in the airport cell phone lot, which is the first turn-off I happen to see. "Really, I'm fine!" I keep yelling. Finally she pulls over and opens the doors. I jump out and hit the ground running, back along the highway toward the convention center. It's probably about a mile or two south of where I am right now.

It's impossible.

Still, I run. It's the only thing I can do. I run until the stitch in my side turns into a needle, and then a sharp dagger. What is wrong with the people who go out for track? This is serious pain!

I start waving madly for a cab—there's got to be cabs,

right? We're near the airport! But no one is stopping.

I know it for sure, now. I'm going to miss the cutoff time.

My feet are killing me. My throat is so parched I can't swallow. I'm sweating and miserable and it stinks like traffic and I'm jumping at every car horn and John Lockdown would say "be strong!" and Liberty would say "relax!"—but they're both full of it. I can't.

It's over.

I stop on the sidewalk, panting, hands on knees.

Suddenly, a car honks. I jump two feet in the air, then turn quickly to see a black convertible, swerving with a screech to the curb. A woman's arm waves wildly. "Hey! What are you doing lollygagging out here on the highway? It's dangerous!"

Red hair! Russian accent! Natasha Romanova!

I mean, Olga. She swerves neatly next to me and opens the passenger door.

"Where you going? Convention center? Need a ride?" she asks.

I practically fall into her car. "How can I thank you?" I say, gasping. "You are the best!"

She laughs, and peels out with a jolt. And just like that, I'm racing toward the finish—in Black Widow's convertible, with the wind in my hair. Laughing.

She drops me right in front of the plaza with minutes to spare. I race to the big gold Trivia Quest platform. There's a much smaller crowd than this morning.

A Quest official taps his microphone. "Last call!" His voice reverberates across the plaza. "Last call to redeem your tokens!"

Six small booths, for the winners of one through six tokens, are closing up shop, or just handing out the last of their consolation prizes. Folks are walking away with bobblehead dolls, key chains, posters, that kind of stuff. Meanwhile, there's a big banner in front of me with the words *ALL 7 TOKENS = VIP PASSES!* written in shining golden letters. I make a mad dash while pulling my coins from of my pack.

It's like it happens in slow motion. Someone comes flying at me from out of left field. Before I can react, I'm hip-checked, hard, on my side.

I go flying.

My seven golden coins go flying, too.

They sparkle in the air in the late afternoon sun.

And behind the airborne, glittering coins, I see the horrified face of Dylan Bustamante, his jaw dropping open as he realizes what he has done.

The coins fall to the ground. They hit the concrete floor of the plaza, spinning and rolling in every direction.

"Dang! Sorry!" says Bustamante.

I'm already on my hands and knees, scrambling to retrieve the coins, dodging under people's feet, this way and that. I grab at a man who's about to pocket one. "Hey, mister, that's mine!" I yell, tugging on his arm. He shrugs and hands it over.

"I found four!" Dylan comes looming toward me out of the sea of people, handing over some tokens. "How many do you have? Do you have them all back?"

One, two, three, four, five, six . . .

One, two, three, four, five, six . . .

44

SIX.

Not seven.

My seventh token is lost.

"LAST CALL!" the announcer shouts.

My lips move, but no words come out. I'm numb.

Joon swats Dylan on the back of the head. "Why'd you knock into him?" he says.

Dylan shrugs. "I was just goofing around! I didn't know what he was holding!"

"Well," I say, my voice more of a croak, "I was holding seven tokens. Now I have six. Six tokens won't get a VIP pass."

Joon and Dylan stare at me solemnly.

"Where's Liberty, by the way?" Joon asks.

"She had to leave early."

"So you've been competing alone?"

I nod. "Just at the end, though."

The loudspeakers boom once more: "*Attention, Questers! The booths will be closing in just a few minutes! Redeem your tokens NOW.*"

I look sadly at the six coins in my hand. It figures that stupid Dylan would ruin this, because stupid Dylan ruins everything.

That's pretty much the story of my life. One minute it's a piece of cake; the next, I'm trapped in a dog crate. One minute, Dad's right there; the next, he's left us. One minute, I'm in elementary school, and I have a best friend. The next minute, I'm at Peavey, silent and alone.

I think of John Lockdown, and the stories on the sketchpad. How he said my superpowers would kick in someday.

And I've been dumb enough to believe it.

Joon and Dylan have moved off a bit, and they're arguing. Joon says something I can't make out. Dylan says, "Chill out already!"

"LAST CALL!" shouts the loudspeaker.

Joon comes over and stands in front of me, scratching his head and frowning. "Stan," he says. "Sorry Dylan bumped you." He opens his hand and shows me his token. "We only got this one. Then we got stumped, and spent the rest of the time goofing around. I mean, don't get me wrong. It was fun. Maybe not as much fun as it would have been with you there with us."

I look up to meet his eyes. But he's still staring at his gold coin. Then, quickly, he grabs my hand and presses it into my palm.

I look from Joon to the coin and back again. Dylan, hovering behind Joon, nods and says "Take it, dude."

"Seriously? Are you sure?"

Joon puts up his hands and backs away. He won't take it back.

"LAST CALL!" comes the voice from the overhead speakers.

I'm frozen, until Joon starts shoving me toward the winners' booth. I look at him, and I can see the old Joon, there, for a change. (That is, once I look past the *Dragon Ball Z* hair.)

"You gotta tell me *everything* about Comic Fest next weekend." Joon punches my arm. "And check for Green Lama stuff."

I nod.

"Now get your scrawny VIP butt up there. They're closing," Joon says.

So I do.

45

BACK IN MRS. Lee's van, rumbling toward home, my brain's too burnt out to process any more sounds, smells, or sights. I close my eyes. I'm done.

But everyone else is super-excited. Dylan's up front, chatting with Mrs. Lee. And here in back, Joon keeps badgering me with questions about the trivia clues and punching my arm. Now he asks, "Hey, can I see them?"

I rub my bruised arm, and hand over the long blue envelopes with the red and gold logo of Comic Fest. He gently touches the giant gold Q embossed on the back.

"Remember that day on Olga's bus?" I ask Joon. "When we first heard the radio ad for the Quest?"

Joon smiles. "And now you won it." He carefully opens an envelope and stares at the shiny card. From the look in his eyes, you'd think it's made of real gold.

Mrs. Lee pipes up from the front seat. "They said not very many Questers found all seven clues today. Congratulations, Stanley Fortinbras!"

"Thanks, Mrs. Lee."

"And I am glad to hear Joon did a generous thing and replaced the token for you." She wags her finger at Joon and Dylan. "That was the right thing to do. Always treat your friends right. Good friends are more valuable than silly tokens."

Joon pretends to gag.

Mrs. Lee keeps on talking. "So, say again: Why did Liberty leave early, Stanley?"

"I don't know. Her mom had some kind of worry-attack about her. She seemed pretty upset . . . I think Liberty's life is kind of complicated."

As we turn down Canyon Rim, Joon hands the VIP passes back, and looks at me squarely. "Well, at least you won, Stan. If I couldn't, I'm glad you did. Hope you and Liberty have a blast next weekend," he says.

I know that look in his eye. It's the same look he had when we were nine, and I got a Power Rangers Super Megaforce Legendary Megazord for my birthday, but he didn't. It's Joon's mega-jealous look.

But you know what? He had his chance to compete with me.

It's not my fault he ditched me for Dylan.

46

THE MINUTE THEY drop me home, I head over to the Silverbergs' and ring the bell. I can't wait to see Liberty's face when I give her the VIP pass. And I want to make sure her mom has calmed down, that whatever happened is over and all is good. I want to tell her how I solved the Superman clue, then got on the wrong bus, but Natasha saved me, but then I lost the token, but then Joon came through for me. . . . So much happened after her mom swooped in and grabbed her.

It takes a long time before I hear footsteps inside the house. Then Dr. Silverberg opens the door. His red hair is sticking up around his bald spot, and his eyes are puffy behind his glasses, like he'd been sleeping.

"Hey, Dr. Silverberg. Could I talk to Liberty? Did her

mom drop her back here yet?"

He frowns and scratches his forehead. "Her *mom*?" Then he opens the door wider to let me in the entry hall. I see books and half-empty moving boxes, their contents still piled on the floor and on the living room couch. "What are you talking about, Stanley?" He looks puzzled. "Isn't she with you?"

We stare at each other for a minute. "No, sir. Her mom came to the Quest and got her about two hours ago, when we were on the next-to-last clue."

Dr. Silverberg's eyes come suddenly into focus. He rushes into the kitchen and picks up his phone.

I tiptoe in behind him. Their kitchen is on the left; ours is on the right. Their house is the exact reverse layout of ours, just like their family. Her folks are the opposite of my parents. And Liberty is the opposite of me.

"Where are you?" Dr. Silverberg shouts into the phone. "But don't you see, you can't just pick her up without telling me—and you just left Stanley there?—I have to be told first—don't you see? That's so impulsive!"

"I understand. You got too worried, you suddenly needed her with you. But she's fine! You knew she was doing fine here. You need to—"

He listens some more, saying "uh-huh, uh-huh." Finally, Dr. Silverberg hangs up. He rubs his hands over his eyes.

I stand there and wait.

"Well, Stanley, it looks like Liberty is on her way up to LA to stay with her mother for a while."

"What? But—why?"

Dr. Silverberg says, "Liberty's mom got worried that she might be feeling sick again. She wanted to be with her."

I think about Liberty's transparent skin, watery eyes. "But she wasn't sick. She just drank too much coffee."

He smiles sadly. "I don't know if Liberty talked to you about her cancer."

A heavy weight of realization starts slowly traveling through my chest. So that's what it was. "Nope," I whisper.

He goes over to his kitchen sink, takes down two glasses from the cupboard, and fills them with water. He hands me one, and we sit at the table.

"About two years ago, she had horrible stomachaches. Her mom thought she was faking, to keep from being put in public school. So she ignored it. Then, when Liberty came to stay with me for a while, I got concerned. We ran tests. It turned out she had a very rare cancer called appendiceal carcinoid. It affected her digestion and hormones."

"Whoa," I say. Which is stupid. I mean, what do you

say to something like that?

I sip my water so I don't say anything else stupid.

"We caught it very early. She had the proper surgery and the very best care. She's lucky. I firmly believe that Liberty is going to be one hundred percent *fine*," Dr. Silverberg says. "Still, as you can imagine, it was a very rotten, horrible couple of years. She's still trying to gain back her weight and strength."

"Wow," I say. "So . . . What about her mom?"

He grimaces. "She feels guilty for missing those early symptoms. So now she thinks Liberty needs to be kept safe all the time, kept where she can watch over her."

He sighs, plays with his water glass. "People deal with stress and worry and love and concern in very different ways, Stanley . . . But holing Liberty away in a quiet room and guarding over her? Not sure that's the right answer. Not for Liberty."

Wow.

As for me, I love to hole away in a quiet room. It's pretty much one of my favorite things.

But I don't tell that to Dr. Silverberg.

That night, I can't sleep, so I knock on Mom's door.

She's in her huge pink bathrobe, her hair and face all messy from sleep. "It's midnight, honey. What's up?"

"Mom. Did you know Liberty had cancer?"

Mom's sleepiness clears from her face in an instant. She nods to herself. "So that's it."

"Why didn't Liberty tell me? It wasn't right, that she didn't tell me."

Mom puts a hand on my shoulder. "Well . . . think of this: Why don't you like the other kids to know why you get so overwhelmed? What's the reason you don't like to talk about your sensory processing disorder?"

I swallow hard.

Mom gives me a hug. "Do you think if people knew, they would look at you differently? Or maybe it just feels private. And that's okay."

I don't say anything, but I get it.

"I think Liberty just wanted you to see *her*, first," Mom says. "There's no right or wrong here, Stanley. It's a personal choice, whether to talk about these things, and with whom, and when. There's no right or wrong to it."

I think about that, as I head back to bed.

47

SUNDAY, THE DAY after the Trivia Quest, I'm like a zombie. I stumble around, and my head feels sick and swirly. I guess it was all the sensory overload.

So I stay in my pajamas and watch the extremely boring history of hydraulics on TV for a while with Gramps, then go back to bed and read comics. Every so often I look at the two VIP passes, which I've pinned to the corkboard on my wall.

"Since Liberty's gone, why don't you offer that second ticket to your brother?" Mom had said when she saw them pinned there. Cal had been right behind her in the hallway, and he immediately fell to the floor and clutched his throat. "Well . . . maybe Joon, then?" she added, swatting at Cal.

I don't want to think about giving Liberty's ticket away to anyone right now. I'm still hoping she comes back.

I fall asleep in my bed, surrounded by comics. When I wake up later in the day, the light's already fading to purple outside my window. Sunday's almost over.

I hear strange bustling downstairs in the kitchen. There are delicious smells wafting around. As I'm sitting up and rubbing my eyes, Mom calls out: "Stanley? We're eating in the dining room tonight! Go wash up!"

I do, and when I come downstairs, Mom, Cal, and Gramps are standing behind their chairs, waiting for me with big grins on their faces.

In the center of the table is a platter of spaghetti and raisin meatballs—my favorite homemade Mom-dinner. Homemade Mom-dinners are rare as comet sightings so this is awesome. And next to the spaghetti is a big round cake that says *Congratulations, Stanley!* On it are seven yellow frosting coins.

There's even a replacement phone, sitting by my place at the table.

It's all so nice, it makes my head feel swirly again.

But not in a sick way. In a really, really, really good way.

Lib: Hey from LA.

Stan: Hey. Everything okay?

Lib: Yup. But I'm sorry. I'm not gonna be back in time for Comic Fest.

Stan: Dang. Well, how's your mom? You feeling okay?

Lib: She's fine, I'm fine, we're fine. Uncle Dan said he told you about my stupid cancer. I guess I should have told you.

Stan: You don't have to talk about it. It's cool.

Lib: GOOD! I'd rather not. For now. So tell me: is Joon taking my ticket? Is he happy?

Stan: Is he happy!? Is the Green Lama a crime-fighting Buddhist?

Liberty: What?

Stan: Never mind. YES, he's excited. And I hope LA is okay. And that everything is cool with your mom . . .

There's a lot more I want to say to her, but I don't know how. Yet.

That next Saturday morning, bright and early, Joon and I are in line to get into Comic Fest's main exhibition hall. We're both jittery with excitement.

Joon's got on his Green Lama cape. Every two seconds, he blurts out, "hey, by the way, thanks," and "wow, really, thank you," and "um, did I say thanks?"

"Thank Liberty, dude," I say, shuffling forward with him in the line. "Not me."

"I know," he says. "I'm just—glad you still want to hang out. I know I've been acting like kind of a jerk."

I don't say anything. But it's nice to hear.

When we get to the front of the line, we're so excited to flash our VIP passes! A big, bored-looking guy waves a wand over us, completely unimpressed. Another one hands us convention booklets, and big freebie tote bags, and boom, we're in.

This is the dream. We. Are. Living. The. Dream. WE'RE AT COMIC FEST!

Famous actors! *Just standing around! Celebrities, standing like ten feet from us!*

And tons of booths filled with vintage comics of every possible era. Fans poring over huge stacks to add to their collections.

Massive lines of people snake around the edges of the hall, waiting to get into special discussion and film screening panels.

I look at my VIP pass. It includes entry into an exclusive lunchtime panel with the Master. Epic!

And the costumes! We look around and see Wonder Women and Obi-Wans, Professor Xs and Magnetos, Hulks and Princess Leias, Batmen and Spider-Men, *Game of Thrones*-ers, Ms. Marvels, and Captain Americas, male and female. And *some* people—whoa—I have *no* clue what they're dressed as. There are a lot of super-sexy costumes, and super-weird ones, too.

And . . . if I wasn't sure it was impossible, I could swear I've just seen someone in a silver-gray jumpsuit and utility belt disappear around a corner, with a swish of a bright blue cape. I crane my neck, frowning.

"What's the matter?" Joon asks. "What are you looking for?"

"I thought—never mind," I say. "Too much to explain."

Joon's goal is to look for vintage Green Lama comics. He's got the hood up on the cloak his mom made him for Halloween two years ago, and he's already been asked twice if he's supposed to be the Green Arrow, which really ticks him off.

I'm not wearing a costume. Too uncomfortable. Plus I have a hard enough time just figuring out how to be myself. I smile, nod, and pretend the roaring noise and pressing crowd don't bug me. But my ears are pounding—despite the fact that I'm wearing a pair of Mrs. Ngozo's earplugs—and my skin's already crawling.

"Isn't this awesome?" Joon asks, and I give two wobbly thumbs-up.

With Liberty, I could complain about the sensory overload. But with Joon, I always need to act cooler than I feel.

The longer we spend wandering around the main exhibit floor, the buzzier my head gets. When Joon tries to talk to me, I can only see his lips moving against the dull roar of the room.

Wait. Did I just see that flash of blue cape again?

No way.

I'm so small, I'm getting knocked and elbowed constantly. It's like people don't even see me down here. They step backward onto me, brush past me. My nose is filled with the smell of fried food and people's deodorant and perfume and body odor, and this weird plastic smell that's maybe coming from the carpet.

"Joon!" I call. "Wait up!" I'm stuck behind some Trekkers—he's gone on without me.

I am sweating in places I didn't even know I had sweat glands, and breathing fast. Wait—there he is! That man in a silver-gray jumpsuit, mask, and blue cape. He's by a Dr. Octopus display, and when he turns slightly, I see that on the front of his thick blue utility belt is a golden buckle with the letters *JL*.

I . . . *drew* that belt! How does it even *exist* in real life?

Okay. I have to make a decision. Do I try to catch up with Joon? Or do I follow this . . . this . . . John Lockdown?

Clearly, I go with the superhero. I dodge left and push right like a robotic tracking drone. Even though the crowd is Blue-Paloma-concert-level thick.

Still, he's getting away! He's slipped between the World of Warcraft booth and a swarm of *Firefly* fans.

I stop.

I take in a giant breath.

I've always been a super-quiet, soft-spoken, stuttering sort of kid. But there's a time and a place for everything.

I shout—so loudly, everyone around me turns:

"IS JOHN LOCKDOWN IN THIS BUILDING??????"

Then I stand there, panting.

Just visible up ahead, I see him—the man in the blue mask and cape. He looks through the crowd at me, and I wave both arms in the air.

Then the crowd shifts again, and he's gone.

48

NOW I'VE LOST both Joon *and* John Lockdown.

I have to get outside for fresh air.

I find a bench, sit, and wait for the buzzing in my ears to settle. I've sat on more benches in more public places lately than ever before in my life. My butt's going to have permanent benchmarks on it, if this keeps up.

I don't know how much time goes by with me in a daze like that. But eventually I'm interrupted by the sound of someone clearing their throat.

"Mind if I sit?"

A man's shape is silhouetted against the bright sun.

A man in a silver-gray jumpsuit.

"Excuse me, but you're the kid—you're from Peavey. Your name is Stanley, right?" John Lockdown asks, bending over me, slightly, with a friendly smile. "You called to me in there, didn't you?"

Am I dreaming?

Am I breathing?

When he sits, his knees crack, and he grimaces. He takes off the mask, and that's when I notice the familiar face. The gray hair.

"Wait—Doc? You're Doc, right? *You're* here at Comic Fest—as John Lockdown?"

He gives me a stiff smile.

"So . . .You were the one drawing stuff back and forth with me on the Sketchpad of Mystery? You?"

Doc the custodian laughs. "Is that what you call it? Sketchpad of Mystery?" He snaps his fingers. "I like it. That's catchy." He sets a black art portfolio next to him on the bench. "That was me. And now, look at me! I'm John Lockdown in the flesh, yes indeed." He wags a finger at me: "Although I don't have a portal at the back of my utility closet. Yet."

I never noticed before—maybe because I never heard him talk before—but Doc has an Irish accent. I break into a huge grin. "I should have figured it might be you! Because of course you'd be in the offices."

He winks. "I was cleaning one night when I saw the markers left out, and I was curious. I opened the sketchpad, and there on the first page, what do I see?

The sketch of a boy trapped inside a burning dog crate. Screaming for help. Now, how could anyone let that go unanswered—a cry for help from a fellow illustrator?"

I feel my face go hot.

"Being a school custodian is my day job, Stanley. But I'm hoping someday to break into comics. Do illustration."

"You're great at it," I say, shyly. "Finding your drawings on the sketchpad every week? That's basically been the only good part of middle school."

"And finding your drawings back to me? Best part of the custodial job. Not counting the paycheck."

"Come on. My drawings are basically stick figures."

"But you have a knack for a story line. YOU created John Lockdown! You took those ridiculously scary safety drills, and turned that around into something new, something positive. A force for good! A superhero!"

He fiddles with the edge of the blue cape, and looks a little embarrassed. "I hope you don't mind that I decked myself out like him. It was just a gimmick, for a meeting."

"Course I don't mind!" I say. "It's so cool to see John Lockdown in real life."

And to know I'm not hallucinating.

And to hear someone else say that they think those safety drills are "ridiculously scary."

John Lockdown—I mean Doc—sighs and stretches

out his legs in their silver tights. "I was hoping to impress a publisher, to get inside a meeting and show my work. But it didn't pan out."

"That's too bad."

"Ah well. It's a tough business." He sighs again.

We sit there, on the bench, in silence for a moment—and then I happen to glance at my entry badge. Which has a sticker on it, reading, *Exclusive Lunch Panel with the Master.*

I get an idea.

There I'm and Doc aren't talking shirt business, but
Mr. Jaye smokes true I'm grinning so wide, nobody's
him.

49

THE SECURITY GOONS don't want to let Doc and me both
into the room on my one VIP pass—until the Master
himself walks over to see what's the matter.

Doc doesn't have to do much beyond open his portfolio and lay out a few quick spreads. The drawings do all
the talking. The Master's bushy eyebrows shoot up when
he sees an amazing drawing Doc did of John Lockdown
stepping into the utility room portal, brandishing his
galactic-super-charged mop and pail.

The Master holds up the pages, one by one, and his
face sort of cracks into this giant smile.

He shakes Doc's hand, then mine. Wait till I tell
Joon!

Then, he and Doc start talking some business stuff.

My face cracks, too. I'm grinning so wide, my cheeks hurt.

50

A WHILE LATER, DOC and I finally make our way back out to the plaza. Joon's lying on a bench, green hood up over his face, two big shopping bags of Comic Fest merchandise at his feet.

I nudge his foot and he jumps. He rubs his eyes, and looks from me to Doc, and back to me. "What the heck, dude? You disappeared. I thought for sure you were having one of your fits so I came out to look for you. I wouldn't blame you. It's so crowded in there."

It is, but I can barely listen to Joon talk—I'm so excited, I'm jumping up and down. Finally, I explode: "Doc and I just pitched John Lockdown Is in the Building to the Master!" I shout. "And he liked it!"

Joon's mouth drops open.

"Well, he said he's going to confirm within a few weeks," Doc adds. "It's a conditional first-level approval."

"That means a trial issue of John Lockdown!" I am practically shaking Joon by the shoulders. "Maybe a whole new superhero series!" I shout. "And it's all because of the Sketchpad of Mystery!"

Joon keeps looking from me, to Doc in his costume, back to me. "Sketchpad of what?" he squeaks. "And what do you mean, John Lockdown? Hey, aren't you that custodian from school?"

Oh, right. Joon's missed out on a lot lately.

51

DOC STAYS WITH us while we wait for Mrs. Lee to come get us. Meanwhile, I fill Joon in on some of the stuff he's missed. The safe room at school. The Sketchpad of Mystery. The back-and-forth cartooning.

"Wow," Joon says. "So, can I see the stuff you drew?"

"Soon," I say. And to Doc, I add, "Joon's into cartooning, too. He's a way better artist than me."

"Really?" says Doc. "Maybe we should look into forming a school cartooning club or something."

"Yesss!" says Joon.

"That'd be great!" I say.

Which is pretty funny, because when Mom suggested I start a comics club, I thought it was the stupidest idea in the world.

When we pull up at my house, I feel like I've been gone for eons. I'm suddenly exhausted. Like I could lie down on my bed and sleep for a year. I get out, thank Mrs. Lee, and head around to the back door—where I hear loud voices. Mom, Gramps, and Cal are standing in the yard by the chicken coop.

"Hey!" I call out to them. "Comic Fest was epic!"

They look up, but no one says a thing. A few more steps forward, and I see why.

One part of the chicken wire is all loose and bent, with a ton of scattered feathers lying around, and dark patches of what I guess is chicken blood. It looks like something pulled our chickens right out from under the sharp wires of the fence.

My stomach squirms like I swallowed a bunch of worms. I think I might throw up.

"They got Henrietta!" Cal shouts it at me, as if it's my fault. "And Chick. And Fil-A!" He waves his arms around. "They snuck right up in broad daylight. I told you so, Mom. I *told* you this coop wasn't secure!"

I try not to look at the bent wire fencing. The rest of the flock struts around our ankles, as if to say, "Hey, when's dinner?" It's a good thing chickens are dumber than Albert Einstein. Hopefully they won't be traumatized.

Mom heads for the workbench in the garage. "Come on, Dad," she says. "Help me fix this."

Cal is glaring at Mom's back. When she's out of earshot, he mutters, "And who's going to fix those stupid coyotes?"

I look at my brother carefully. His fists are clenched, and his face is bright red.

"Why are you so obsessed with the coyotes, Cal?" I ask.

He jerks his head back, like I'm an idiot for even asking. "The chickens are one thing. You know they could also gang up and kill Albert Einstein, right? One of them sneaks behind and slits his hamstrings, while the others distract him. Then they close in for the kill. That's how they take down the bigger dogs. And Albert Einstein's so dumb and trusting—he'd just stand there and let them. We shouldn't ever let him out of the house by himself. Not ever."

Cal's breathing is ragged. "Look at the chicken coop. It's a disaster. And it's Mom's fault." He runs his hands through his hair. "Everything is."

"Everything is Mom's fault?" I repeat.

"All she does is work. Everything around here is falling apart. Dad's not around to check on stuff, like he used to. Gramps can't help." Cal glares at me. "She shouldn't have let Dad go away. She should have stopped him."

His words feel like they're twisting around in my chest. For the first time, I see how scared Calvin is. How much he misses Dad, too. But his way is to get angry.

"I miss him, too," I say. "But how is it Mom's fault? Maybe she has to work so hard to make more money because Dad's stupid new job means he can't send as much. Did you ever think of that?"

Cal kicks at the broken pile of chicken wire. "Figures you're on her side," he mutters. "Mommy's precious Stannie." Then he stalks into the house.

I had been feeling so great when Mrs. Lee dropped me home. So happy about Comic Fest, and Doc.

Wow—it took like two minutes for it all to go south.

52

I SIT AT SUNDAY dinner in a kind of trance.

It's been a lot for me. The sensory onslaught of Trivia Quest, then a busy week of school, then the sensory onslaught of Comic Fest. The whole excitement about Doc, and John Lockdown, and then the big chicken disaster. Plus I lost Liberty, just when we'd gotten to be friends.

"Your chin's practically hanging in your soup dish, Stanley," Mom says, giving me her patented laser Look. "You need a recharge. I'm letting you stay home tomorrow."

So I get to spend Monday in bed, surrounded by glorious silence—only broken by the muffled sounds of Gramps's TV. I sleep off and on, and stare at the painted planets, floating off-kilter on my walls. It's nice.

Stan: Hey, Liberty.

Lib: Heya, Stan.

Stan: Where are you, exactly?

Lib: Still L.A.

Stan: I mean where are you living? Everything okay with your mom?

Lib: Well sure, she's happy, now that I'm stuck here under her thumb 24/7. Ugh. We're staying with her new boyfriend. Mom says once she finds a better job, we'll get our own place and it'll get better.

Stan: What about you?

Lib: I'm good. I can walk to a library. The boyfriend is all right. LA's cool . . .

Okay, now Liberty, she's been through cancer. And a wild, weird, moving-around life, where nothing stays the same for long. And a mom who seems really unpredictable. She doesn't even have a regular school to go to.

I don't think I could deal with all that. I'd be having Red Alerts all over the place, all the time.

But nothing ever seems to get to Liberty Silverberg. How does she manage that superhero trick?

53

ON TUESDAY, it's actually kind of nice to be back at school. Mrs. Green is in a good mood, Kyle Keefner's absent, and there are no surprise drills.

During lunch, Doc, Joon, and I meet with Principal Coffin to get permission for a comic art club.

"I could teach 'em the writing, storyboarding, penciling, inking, lettering, coloring—that is, if they want," Doc says, sliding our Sketchpad of Mystery across the desk so Principal Coffin can see it.

She puts on thick reading glasses and makes a big show of examining the drawings. The big old wall clock behind her ticks loudly. It makes me think of the clock at Horton Plaza.

"You and young Stanley, here? You created this

John Lockdown character?" She peers up at us, over her glasses. "From *my* secret safety code phrase? You've lifted, and revealed, the secret Peavey code phrase?" She frowns. "I thought I made it clear that the phrase was to remain a school secret."

I feel my cheeks start to burn. Doc fidgets with his pencil. Would she fire him for something like that?

"It's my fault," I hear myself blurting out. "I was just writing down thoughts on the pad, you know, and I was wishing for—I don't know. Something good to come out of all the horrible, scary drill stuff. A superhero that could . . . protect me."

It sounds so stupid when I say it out loud. Joon looks kind of shocked. And did I just call our principal's safety program "horrible, scary drill stuff"?

There's a long silence. Principal Coffin frowns even harder and says: "What do you mean, exactly, by *horrible, scary drill stuff*?" She makes a point of crossing her arms. Her forehead's full of puckered, wrinkled lines.

Oh, boy.

"I didn't mean to be rude. I mean, the drills are good. It's good to be safe. I get it. But sometimes . . ."

"Sometimes what?" She leans forward.

"Sometimes they totally go overboard with too much drama. Like, totally over the top. It's awful! Ma'am."

She gasps. Joon gasps. Doc takes a small step back

toward the door.

"I mean—I know they're necessary. But always being reminded about all these terrible things that could happen any minute at school? I just can't handle that level of impending doom."

I shrug, and look down at the floor. I hold my eyes wide so no one notices there are tears forming in them.

I'm a wimp. Just like Cal says. And now I've gone and insulted the principal. It just all came rushing out of nowhere! She'll hate me now. With three years of middle school left to go.

Principal Coffin gets up from her chair. She comes out from behind her desk and stands over me, frowning harder than ever, hands on her wide hips.

And then she bends down and puts her hands on my shoulders.

"Thank you, Stanley," she says. Her eyes are giant and misty behind her reading glasses. "Here I thought I was just spicing things up, to make it fun for the kids! Telling me how you really feel about it? That was brave, Stanley. And I appreciate it."

I just know Joon is smirking like crazy, standing behind me.

"So what do you think about the comics club idea?" Doc says softly.

Principal Coffin smiles—and nods.

54

Lib: How was the first club meeting?

Stan: Bad. We have to advertise better. Dylan Bustamante was the only one who showed. And Joon still acts stupid around him.

Lib: How so?

Stan: They had a spitting contest into the garbage pail every time Doc wasn't looking. I'm still kind of mad at Joon. I thought since I took him to Comic Fest, maybe he'd change back to the old Joon.

Lib: People don't change back—or stay the same. Not even you. And if Joon wants to spit, he's gonna spit.

Stan: It's not all bad. It's just not like before. How about you?

Lib: Well, Mom keeps flubbing auditions. The only acting she's doing is acting upset. And a breakup's coming with the boyfriend.

Stan: Bummer!

Lib: She knows this theater company in Portland. We might go there.

Stan: Portland, Oregon?

Lib: Portland, Maine.

Stan: Ouch. That's far . . .

Lib: Yup.

55

THE PAST TWO Saturdays have been epic—first Trivia Quest, then Comic Fest. But I'm super happy that this Saturday is back to being a normal one. A calm one. A lazy one. A hang-out-at-home-and-vegetate-into-a-stupor Saturday.

Gramps is parked in his recliner, watching a show about doomsday preppers. They're these people who think the world's ending so they stock up on ammo and make all these elaborate warlike preparations.

I can only handle watching it for a few minutes. "This is awful!" I tell Gramps. "I mean, there's a million ways the world could end. How are they gonna prepare for all those possibilities? Canned goods and firearms? I'm having a panic attack. Seriously, it's worse than sitting through a Principal Coffin safety assembly."

He says, "I tell you, Stanley, I been in the war, you know. The world can get crazy out there. People cope in different ways." Then he lets out a huge belch of lunchtime hot dog. Ugh. Albert Einstein lunges into his lap and sniffs, making Gramps wave his arms and legs around wildly. "Dang dog! Get him the heck out of here!"

I grab Albert Einstein by the collar and try to wrestle him up with me to my room to do homework, but he slips back down to stay with Gramps. Fine.

Ten minutes later, there's some sort of wild commotion with Gramps shouting again. He's always yelling at the TV, so at first, I ignore it. But then, there's a shout so sharp and strange, I come running.

Mom, Cal, and I all get to the living room at about the same time.

Gramps is moaning on the floor by his chair, while Albert Einstein whines at him. "Stupid fool of a dog jumped right in front of me when I was getting up. Dang it, I think I dislocated my bum shoulder again!"

Uh-oh.

"Oh, Dad!" Mom cries out. "Not again! Stanley, get the ice pack." Meanwhile, she runs for the first aid kit. She bandages Gramps's arm to his body to keep it from moving around. She's gotten good at this—he's dislocated it before.

"Let's get you to the hospital for an x-ray," she says. "Boys? Hold down the fort! Fend for yourselves for dinner if we're not home!"

As Mom helps a wincing Gramps to the car, she's still shouting directions back at us. "Cal, find yourself another ride to football practice! Stanley, fold the laundry. And order a pizza or something. Lord knows how long we'll be. Oh my gosh wait a sec, let me help you with that seat belt, Dad."

"Fend for ourselves," Calvin mutters. "What else do we ever do around here?"

"Aren't you worried about Gramps?" I ask.

"Of course I am, stupid." Cal opens the fridge and stares gloomily at the empty shelves. "But it's not the first time he popped that shoulder out. He'll live."

I leave him in the kitchen and go to my room. Albert Einstein follows me, head down, his toenails click-clicking obediently on the stairs, like he knows he did something bad.

I'm working on some John Lockdown comics to show Doc. Not the drawings so much as the story lines. I want to be in on the action when the Master tells Doc he'll publish John Lockdown for real.

Also, Principal Coffin wants the school paper to run

a *John Lockdown* comic strip. She's totally bought into the idea—she thinks "our school superhero could offer kids helpful safety tips of what to do in a crisis!"

So I'm scribbling away when I notice Calvin clomping around in the hall.

"Don't you have football practice?"

"Not today," he grunts.

I hear him go into Mom's room, which is a little weird—then downstairs to the kitchen. A minute later, the back door slams.

I'm just starting to really get into this John Lockdown story line when a loud cracking noise comes from the backyard.

Albert Einstein hurls himself downstairs like a rocket, toenails scratching and slipping, barking like crazy.

Above the barking comes this strange howl. At first I think: a coyote. But then the howl turns into a human scream.

My brother's scream.

I fly downstairs and out the back door. "Cal?" I yell, scanning the yard.

The chickens are flustered, flapping around in their coop.

I spot Cal in the far back corner of our yard, where it slopes down to the canyon. I gasp when I see what he's holding. So that's what he was doing, banging around up in Mom's room. He was searching for that rifle!

Apparently, he found it.

He sways in place. Then he drops.

I run, skidding in the rocks and sand, and stop at the edge of the slope.

Cal is sitting on the ground now. As I get closer, I see some blood oozing out of his sneaker. Not some. A lot of blood.

My heart starts pounding full force. Red Alerts pang through me at top speed and pressure—my stomach's a pit of writhing snakes—oh no—oh no—

—But somehow, I'm not sinking to the ground like

Cal. No. Instead, I'm in a hyper state of super-alertness. "Don't move!" I shout. "I'm going to . . ."

I stop and think.

I'm going to . . . what?

Calvin's eyes roll around in his head. He lays all the way down, pale as a ghost.

I'd give anything right now to see John Lockdown streaking through the air toward us, ready to take charge. John Lockdown, or anyone—Wonder Woman, Batman, X-Men, Avengers, Captain America, Agent Carter, Iron Man—heck, I'll take Mighty Mouse.

But no one's coming to the rescue. There's only me.

Whipping off my T-shirt, I wrap it around his bloody foot, and press. *Compression.* That's the word. That's what you're supposed to do. Then, looking around, I see a plastic bucket by the chicken coop—I pull it over and prop Cal's leg up. Somehow, in the back of my brain, from one of Principal Coffin's assemblies before I started going to my Ready Room, I remember you're supposed to raise the wounded part up.

It's been maybe thirty seconds, and my T-shirt, wrapped around his foot, is already soaked through. The blood looks like the red that seeps from packages of raw steak.

Cal sits up again, trying to peel away the bloody shirt and look. "No! Just hold it tight and don't move!" I command him in a deep voice that doesn't even sound like me.

I run inside and call 911. Then I race next door, but Dr. Silverberg's not home. I race back to Cal with a stack of kitchen towels. I press down hard on the wound. *Compression*. It's bleeding like crazy.

"Lie back!" I tell Cal as he scrambles to sit. "Stay down on the grass and breathe. Deep, from your stomach. In, out, from your belly. Breathe slowly. What's your favorite color?"

He looks at me like I'm crazy, before he passes out.

56

WAAAAH, WAAAAH, WOOP, goes the siren, and then it's in our actual driveway, and the back doors swing open. Two medics in blue scrubs come toward us. "Here!" I shout, waving my arms like a frantic windmill. "He's over here!"

"Talk to us." One of the medics squats down by Cal. He has big sideburns like Wolverine. His partner, an older lady with a crew cut and huge arms, is already checking Cal's blood pressure and stuff.

I tell them everything. I feel like I'm standing next to my body, watching myself acting like a calm person. I tell them all the facts, finishing with his allergies to penicillin and aspirin. Oh yeah, he had his appendix out when he was ten.

The EMT lady clutches my shoulder and looks me in

the eye. "You did good, kid," she says. "You did all the right things. Not many people could keep their cool like that."

I nod, but I barely hear her words, I'm so numb.

Once I'm in the ambulance, with Cal in the back on an orange plastic stretcher, they let me call Mom on their phone. But when I hear her voice, I lose it. I hand the phone back to Wolverine, and he explains the whole situation.

"I have to say," he adds, before hanging up, "props to Stanley here. You've got a pretty brave kid."

I'd say thanks, but I'm too busy throwing up in a bucket.

57

IN THE ER, they wheel Calvin behind a curtain, and tell me to stay in the waiting room until my mother gets there.

The waiting room is bad. Sticky plastic chairs, people coughing. It's worse than the Metro bus. Thank God it's only a few minutes before Mom rushes in and hugs me.

"I was just upstairs with your grandfather! What on earth is happening?" she shrieks.

Then she sprints down the hall to find a nurse.

Gramps ambles in a little later. He's got his arm in a tight black sling, and he eases himself into the plastic seat next to mine with a groan, propping his cane on the armrest. He smells a little funky—it's been a rough day. "Well, here we are, Stanley," he says, staring at the TV bolted onto the wall. "What in heck was your fool brother thinking? See, this is the very reason why your mother should've let me teach him to shoot."

"Or it's the reason you shouldn't have given him that stupid gun in the first place, since Mom didn't even want you to," I say.

"When did you get so full of sass?" Gramps mutters, clicking the channel to something about mega-tornadoes.

We don't talk much after that.

An hour later, Mom comes back. "Calvin's having foot surgery," she says, plopping down in the nearest plastic chair and rubbing at her eyes. "The bullet nicked a toe bone, and they need to check an artery and do cleanup. But he's lucky. It's just minor. He should be fine."

Gramps juts his stubbly chin toward Mom. "I'll tell you something. Your brothers were all wild hellions, but even they'd never have pulled a stupid stunt like Cal's today." He sits back and crosses his arms. "This has to do with his father being missing, here at a what-you-call critical juncture in the young boy's life."

Mom sits up very straight. She looks really pale. "I'm not talking about this," she says to Gramps, carefully pronouncing every word. "I'm calling a cab to take you home."

Gramps looks at me like I'm with him on this. But I'm not.

I mean, I can see ways in which they're both right. Mom's right about the gun being stupid, and deadly dangerous in the hands of someone as dopey as Cal.

And Gramps is right about Dad not being here when we need him.

58

Stan: Liberty, why don't you ever worry about anything?

Lib: Because I dunno. Well, maybe because I have no expectations. Then you're not disappointed when stuff doesn't happen.

Stan: Still don't get it. Don't you worry? For me, it's like a trap I can't avoid.

Lib: But think about the stuff you've handled. The Quest. The Fest. Cal's stupid foot. You're a hero! THE WORRY-TRAP IS IN YOUR MIND.

Stan: So how do I get it *out* of my mind?

Lib: Eh! Don't ask me. Go ask John Lockdown.

59

EVEN THOUGH IT'S super-late when the cab drops us home from the hospital, I can't sleep.

Gramps, on the other hand, took painkillers for his shoulder, and he's been snoring for hours.

I stay up.

At one point in the night, I hear the coyotes again, faint and far away. I shudder.

But then I imagine John Lockdown, flying tight circles around the house, weaving an invisible force field so nothing can get through to hurt us.

It's well past sunrise when the sound of Mom's car in the drive wakes me. I scramble outside to help.

Mom reaches in the car for a set of crutches as Cal

slowly emerges from the backseat. He's got a huge black plastic cast on—it looks like the boot from my old toy Megazord. He stands, shakily, then takes the crutches from Mom. It takes ten minutes for the three of us, hobbling and wobbling, to get him safely inside the house.

"Thank you, Stan," says Mom as my brother sits heavily in Gramps's recliner. We prop his Megazord boot up, and he moans. It's a soft moan, sort of like those midnight coyotes.

"I'll have to make up a bed on the couch for him," Mom says, rubbing her temples, trying to think. "No stairs for a while. I've already ordered the wheelchair . . ."

"You rest. I'll do the couch," I say.

Mom's skin is so pale, she looks waxy. She slumps into a chair and covers her face. When a good five minutes have gone by and she hasn't moved, I go over. "Mom?" I put a hand on one of her shoulders. "Don't worry, Mom. Everything'll be just fine."

She laughs a little, and puts her hand over mine. "Yeah?" she says. "I never thought I'd hear *you* say that, Stanley."

60

ALL THE NEXT week at school, Cal's eighth-grade friends come up and talk to me. Everyone wants to know about him. How's he doing? How did it happen? When will he walk again? When will he be back? Will he play football again? He was—is—was—pretty good at football.

There are rumors going around, too. Dylan heard he did hand-to-hand combat with the coyote. Keefner thought they had to amputate his foot.

Olga the bus driver gave me a get-well card for him, with a pamphlet on gun safety inside.

And Principal Coffin stopped me in the hall to say she heard I acted quick and maybe saved Cal's life.

Wow.

The truth is, Cal is doing fine. He's slowly getting

around, getting better. He'll probably be back to school soon.

When Friday comes, I'm glad for two reasons: the week's almost over, and it's time for comics club. Last week it was only Joon and Dylan and me. But this week Doc had us do a major advertising push. We put up flyers and a big notice in the school paper. I'm wondering who will show.

We wait anxiously in our room as kids bustle past on the way to the bus. Doc hung his John Lockdown costume on a hanger by the door, just to attract attention, and the blue cape wafts in the breeze with all the movement in the hall.

Eventually, two seventh-grade boys hesitate in the doorway. They've got long shaggy hair and plaid flannel shirts, and they give us quick nods as they grab the farthest-away seats. Doc hands them each a pad of paper and a pencil.

Then this eighth-grade girl arrives. Darcy. I know her by sight, because she's the one who designed the mural by the library media center. She's really good. She's got short black hair with a bright blue streak in it, and thick black eyeglasses.

We wait a few more minutes, but it looks like the six of us are going to be it. That's double our numbers from last week—not too bad.

Doc pairs us up for a project. Joon and Dylan push their desks right together. And the two new seventh graders are already in a huddle.

That leaves me with Darcy.

At first, we just look at each other suspiciously. But then, I tell myself that I can do this thing. If I could talk to Liberty, then I maybe I can talk to this girl.

"Hey, Darcy," I say softly. "What about a story about a girl who, after she heals and recovers from this terrible plague, gains these amazing superpowers? But her family, they're overprotective and refuse to let her out of their sight. They lock her away, so she has to escape, out into the night, every night."

There is a flicker of interest in her eyes. "How does she escape?" Darcy asks.

"She climbs out the window into a tall tree that looks out over everything. The town, the ocean. Everything."

"Okay," she says. "What then?"

"So she flies around town saving people. Everyone thinks she's fragile. They don't realize that she is really made of steel, with superstrength. This girl, she can handle stuff."

Darcy loves the idea.

She's drawing the girl to look like her. We're calling the comic *Blue Streak*.

Doc asked me if I wanted to think about a comic featuring a boy with sensory processing disorder and supersensitive senses that lead him into adventures.....

I told him I'm not ready to tackle that story yet.

But maybe soon.

268

61

THE FOLLOWING FRIDAY, at comics club, Doc clears his throat. "Well, troops, I finally got an email back from the Master."

My pencil stops in midair.

"They've signed on for one issue of *John Lockdown Is in the Building*. If they like it—and it's a big if—then maybe—*maybe*—they might order more. Still, this is great news!"

"Wow!" Darcy shouts.

"Cool!" says Joon.

The two seventh graders slap five. Doc is grinning. I'm so proud I think I might burst.

"Yesss! Chest bump!" says Dylan. No one gives him one.

When Mom picks me up after school, she's smiling, too. "Guess who just called me from the airport?" she asks.

"So . . . is Dad coming home?" I ask, nervous to hear her answer.

"Yup. For a few weeks, anyway. Long enough some quality time together. He'll be back tomorrow night." She flashes a quick glance at me. "He's worried about Cal's foot, of course. And he wants to hear all about your comic book contest exploits, Stanley. Lots to catch him up on."

Dad, home . . . Wow. I can hardly remember what that's like. It almost seems like part of a past life.

But that's okay. Because my present life has been going along okay these days. Cal's been way quieter and calmer. School's okay. And now there's comics club.

If only Liberty were around. But nothing's perfect.

To top off all this good stuff, a four-day weekend, thanks to teachers' conference, is about to start. Four days of relaxing, sleeping in, and goofing off . . .

And starting tomorrow night—Dad time.

The next morning, right after breakfast, the doorbell rings. Joon and Dylan walk in like it's no big deal.

"We thought we'd come hang out. You know, since it's Saturday," Joon says, taking off his jacket. "Since

Saturdays are traditionally kind of our thing. Right?"

"Yeah, thanks for having us," says Dylan.

"Um, okay," I say, trying to act like this is no big deal.

We go up to my room. Dylan tries throwing a tennis ball for Albert Einstein, who lets the ball bounce off the top of his head. "I hate to break it to you, but I don't think your dog's very smart," Dylan says.

"Four days off! Maybe we can go to the comics store. Or the movies, or the mall," Joon says, giving me a careful glance.

"Yeah, maybe one or two of those things," I say. "If I space it out with some downtime."

"It's a deal," Joon says, punching my arm.

Out the window, I see Gramps in the yard, feeding the chickens. He's got plans for a new, state-of-the-art, doomsday-proof, coyote-secure chicken facility. Once Dad gets home tonight, we're all going to start building. Even Cal said he'd help.

While Dylan tries to play ball with Albert Einstein, and Joon listens to music, I glance at my phone. There's a text from Liberty, with a photo this time—she's standing by her mom, and they have their arms around each other. They have the same exact smile, the same big green eyes. And Liberty's got on a green T-shirt that says *What doesn't kill you makes you stronger. Except for bears. Bears will kill you.*

Lib: Theater job's a go. We're moving to Maine.

Stan: That's bad news! Or is it?

Lib: I've never been to Maine, so how would I know?

Stan: You gonna find a tree to climb, so you can see the other ocean?

Lib: Yeah, and my mom might even let me do it. She's loosening up a bit. And I'll be back, of course. So . . . Trivia Quest, next year: Do we have a date?

Stan: You bet.

Lib: And mail me a copy of the John Lockdown comic, will you? Also, that Blue Streak thing you're doing with Darcy.

Stan: Will do.

Liberty: I can't wait to see all the new stuff you come up with this year, Stanley Fortinbras.

I smile to myself as I put down the phone. And pick

up a pencil. And open my sketchpad.

I guess I might as well begin.

[acknowledgments TK]